Khmer Legends

DEMAZ TEP BAKER

Outskirts Press, Inc.
Denver, Colorado

Outskirts Press, Inc.
http://www.outskirtspress.com

ISBN: 978-1-4327-3937-9

Outskirts Press and the "OP" logo are trademarks belonging to Outskirts Press, Inc.

PRINTED IN THE UNITED STATES OF AMERICA

For my grand daughter Lucia.

Contents

Preface vii

NEANG KANG REI MOUNTAIN

Phnom Neang Kang Rei......................................1

THE POND OF THE HIDDEN PLOUGH

Trapang Lak Neangkal 9

MALE AND FEMALE MOUNTAINS

Phnom Pros Phnom Srey 17

THE STORY OF BATTAMBANG....................21

THE STORY OF PROHM BACHEY

Vat Nokor BaChey 27

THE CROCODILE NEN THON

Krapoeu Nen Thon..37

THE STORY OF THMENH CHEY

(He Always Had The Last Word) 43

THMENH CHEY AT THE PALACE................53

THMENH CHEY ON HIS DEATH BED.................77

RABBIT, THE LAWYER

SOPHEA TONSAY..79

RABBIT AND THE JACKAL 83

RABBIT AND THE TIGER............................89

RABBIT, THE JUDGE 95

RABBIT WANTS TO EAT BANANAS 99

THE DEBTOR AND THE CREDITOR...................101

THE STORY OF TWO DEER HUNTERS 105

THE DREAM...109

Sources and Acknowledgements 113

Glossary...115

Preface

Storytelling was the vital source of sustainability in a desolate place where people were mostly illiterate. It's a form of entertainment or relaxation in the evenings after a hard day's work in the fields. A storyteller was always welcome. I remember the days when my father was head of a small town. Every now and then he invited a well-known storyteller from the neighboring village to recite amazing stories at the compound where we lived. Sometimes it took two or three nights to finish the story. By sundown, everyone, accompanied by all their family members, arrived at the designated place. Mats and blankets were spread on the grass under the moonlit night. Some brought pillows for their children to sleep. It was a cherished moment to be remembered. Seated on an elevated platform, so everybody could see him, the storyteller usually had a homemade guitar with which he played along as he sang and recited his epic story until the wee hours of the morning. Skillful storytelling is an art. Not only did the storyteller possess an amazing memory to record thousands and thousands of lines, he also delighted the audience with vivid gestures and deep feeling that brought tears or laughter to the audience.

Folktales, recounted through this oral tradition, stem from lack of a written language or illiteracy in the past. The only way to pass on folktales was through storytellers. Ironically, when they passed away, they took with them these wonderful stories and the art of telling them. This book tries to remedy this.

Back in the early ages, it was believed that God created the sky, the earth, human beings, and animals. He created many, many other things to fill the earth. He separated the kingdoms and gave them to men. He created races. It was also believed that men and animals could converse with one another. Legends, passed on from generation to generation, put emphasis on supernatural or mythical beings called "Prohms" or "Preah Entrea" from the heavens, who could transform themselves into human beings and make miracles. They could make rains, storms, sunshine, and darkness, among other things. They could move from one world to another. Another fairy-tale figure, representative of kindness, wisdom, and knowledge appeared time and time again in these folktale stories. It was a hermit, a religious figure, called "Ta Eisei." He could teach all who needed to learn to become a great warrior or a great king. He always came to rescue people in distress. On the other hand, creatures like "Giants," representative of naughtiness, trouble, and wickedness, could change their ugly forms into good-looking human beings, or into small animals or insects, whatever they needed to be. They could fly at lightning speed from kingdom to kingdom. They could transform land into water and vice versa. They could move or lift mountains from one end to another. They seemed to possess supernatural powers, and could appear and disappear as fast as they came in. A female giant like Neang Kangrei could become a beautiful human princess and be married to a human prince.

Khmer people in remote rural areas are great believers in these spirits, whereas more sophisticated city people are inclined to believe in science and real medicine. Khmer people also believed in bad spirits and good spirits, called "Neak Ta." Evil spirits could cause sickness. They could enter a body; therefore, they must be called out to cure the patient. Offerings of food and drink were often required to soothe their anger or relieve pain or illness. It was done by a special ritual, a gathering of family members and other believers. Sometimes the whole village attended. Some came to watch out of curiosity, some to lend support. The majority were great believers. The victim was placed in the center of the scene covered with a white cloth. The candles and incense sticks were lit. Food and alcoholic drinks were brought in. It was widely believed that the spirits liked consuming alcoholic drinks. At the beating of a drum or the sound of some melodious musical instruments, the spirits, who could be of either gender, would enter the body of a believer. Usually a woman "received the call." She alone could communicate with the spirits. She alone had the power to mediate between the dead and the ordinary mortals. She began by singing and dancing, gradually increasing the sound of her voice, impersonating some unknown invisible spirits. At times, she burst into a loud satanic laughter, a groan, a moan, or shrieking screams of anger. She swayed to the rhythm of the music, faster and faster, as she increasingly entered a trance motion. She would tell the audience whom she represented and why she was happy or angry. Sometimes she spit betel nut chew over the body of the victim. She had the audience under her complete control. They were subdued and fearful of her shenanigans because she alone could talk to the souls of the dead on behalf of the living. They listened with intensity, their hands joined in obedience, asking for forgiveness. They wanted to please the spirits and would comply with her demands. The session usually ended when she was completely exhausted from the trance. On many occasions, she passed out. When she recovered from her fainting, she did not have any recollection of what had happened.

There were two distinct groups of folktales: war and people folktales (such as Ramayana), and animal folktales. Children loved animal stories. Through these stories that were passed on from mouth to mouth, they felt a close friendship with them, specifically the rabbits, although the latter were sometimes hunted down for their delicious meat.

Animals represented a part of everyday life beliefs. Some black bird cries called "Kleng Srak" would bring bad luck, or even death to the family, if they perched on a tree nearby the house. Black snakes and bees were also considered bad omens. To get rid of these portentous warnings, monks would be invited to chant and spray blessed waters on the family, the house, and the surroundings. Some animals were considered not too intelligent or intelligent but slow, such as tigers and cows. It was not a flattering epithet to be called "Akor" (Kor means cow in Khmer). It's an insult to call someone a dog. Monkeys represented wickedness and lack of seriousness. They played tricks on people. Snakes were considered insincere, dishonest, unworthy. Bulls symbolized simple energy and strength. However, one of the most beloved animal tales was about the rabbit, called "Tonsay" in Khmer. The rabbit story was one of the most frequently told stories, as you will see in later chapters of this book. The rabbit animal was a symbol of great skill, intelligence, cleverness, and decision-making capabilities. The rabbit stories in this book seem to depict or typify the exploitation of the poor by wealthy people of influence, or the weak by the stronger ones. Although social injustice cannot be totally eradicated, logic, fairness and equity usually prevail. The rabbit with its intelligence, shrewdness and its ability to trick the adversaries into total obedience -- sometimes verging on stupidity -- has captured Khmer children. Everyone wants to be a rabbit. It was believed that children born under the sign of the rabbit are clever, smart, and have good luck in general. My recent trip to the rural areas of Cambodia -- after thirty three years -- has not altered my feeling that these beliefs still exist.

NEANG KANG REI MOUNTAIN
Phnom Neang Kang Rei

The province of **Kampong Chhnang** is very well known for its famous mountains that rise majestically on the bank of the river, a tributary of Tonlé Sap, or Great Lake. To reach the river, one can either ride a bicycle, take a pedicab, or drive to the Lower Market, called **Psar Krom**. From there, you can see the two mountains, covered by thick vegetation, side by side across the river. On the lower valley of the mountains, a special aromatic herb, cumin, or in Khmer **Ma Aum** grows in abundance. In other parts of Cambodia, this cumin or Ma Aum is very much sought after to enhance the taste of a special sour soup, **Samlar Machuu**. However, Kampong Chhnang's inhabitants do not use this herb, because it represents the pubic hair of **Neang Kang Rei**, the daughter of an ogress, who is the main character of this folktale. The two mountains represent Nang Kang Rei's breasts as she lay down and died on the bank of the river. Near the mountains there are two villages. These two villages, **Kompong Leng** (Leaving River) and **Kompong Hao** (Calling River), got their names from this story.

If one climbs one of the mountains, one can see a giant mortar and a pestle. Nobody knows, for sure, when, where and how they were put there. The story is that before settling down in this region, newcomers must find the mortar and the pestle, and perform the ritual of pounding the rice. Then the spirit **Nak Ta**, who guards the mountains, will help them defeat all diseases that infest this area, and they will have a long and happy life.

What follows is the story of how these mountains and rivers were formed.

Once upon a time, there lived a very wealthy businessman called "**Sathei.**" He and his beautiful wife did not have any children. One day, they both decided to make some offerings to the spirit (or Nak Ta in Cambodian), that lived under a sacred tree, **Doeum Chhrey**. They had their servants prepare many dishes, including chicken, pork, beef, vegetables, drinks, and abundant fruit. Both husband and wife took the offerings to the "Nak Ta," and asked the spirit to provide them with healthy children.

Soon after, Lok Sathei (Mr. Sathei) and his wife were blessed with twelve beautiful girls. They both loved their daughters very much and lived happily for a while. Suddenly, Sathei lost all his fortune, so that he and his wife were no longer able to provide food for their beloved children. Every night, Sathei and his wife tried to find a way to overcome this insoluble problem.

"We are no longer able to raise our children," Sathei said to his wife. "There is no solution but to abandon them, but I am sure that the Nak Ta who helped us have these children will look after them," Sathei continued.

After many nights of sadness and tears, his wife finally gave in. With broken hearts, Sathei and his wife took their children deep into the forest and, while the children were asleep, abandoned them there. At sunrise, when the twelve girls woke up, and noticed the disappearance of their parents, they all burst into tears. They ran in every direction looking for their parents. Soon, exhausted from crying and running around, their hearts full of sorrow and despair, they abandoned their search and moved on. They walked all day, feeding themselves with fruit and any edible plants found on their way. When they were tired, they looked for a big tree that could protect them from the heat, the wind, and the rain, so that they might rest until they regained enough strength to pursue their journey. After months and years, they arrived at one kingdom of the ogress queen **Yak Santhomear**. This ogress queen had a daughter named **Neang Kang Rei**. When the ogress Santhomear saw the twelve girls, she transformed herself into a beautiful woman and offered to provide them with food and shelter. Seduced by Santhomear's sweet and alluring speech, the girls agreed to follow her. Santhomear took them to her palace and gave them to her daughter, Neang Kang Rei, as servants instead.

When the girls learned that Queen Santhomear was really an

ogress, they were so frightened that they decided to escape. As soon as darkness fell upon the city, they quietly tiptoed out of their quarters and ran into the forest. They kept walking day and night, through thick forests full of dangers and roamed by ferocious animals. They stopped only to sleep in the branches of trees, and to find something to eat to still their hunger.

Finally, they arrived at another kingdom ruled by a human King, **Preah Bat Roth Sothi.** Exhausted, they took refuge under a big tree at the outskirts of the kingdom and prepared themselves for a long nap. Meanwhile, Preah Bat Roth Sothi, his ministers, troops, and servants were hunting. It was a very hot day. The heat was almost unbearable. Around noon, the king called his people for a midday lunch and a little rest. They came upon the tree where the twelve girls were napping peacefully. Although their clothes were ragged, the girls were still very beautiful. Seeing them in such a state, the king took pity on them. He summoned his ministers and servants and ordered them to take the twelve girls to his palace, with orders that perfumed baths, beautiful clothes, and jewels be given to them. After they were fed and clothed, they were taken to the king's private quarters. The new outfits, coupled with exquisite jewels and coiffures, had transformed these girls into heavenly maidens, so that they resembled the lovely **Apsaras** who reside in heaven. Their beauty enchanted the king who immediately fell in love with all of them and took them as his wives.

In the meantime, Santhomear, having discovered the disappearance of the girls, sent her troops looking for them. When the troops brought back the news that the twelve girls had become the king's wives at the other kingdom, Santhomear flew into a rage. She was determined to destroy them. That night she transformed herself into a beautiful woman, more beautiful than any of the twelve girls, and set out to meet the king. Preah Bat Roth Sothi fell in love with Santhomear when he saw her. Without hesitation he asked her to be his wife, and she accepted. After a few months, Santhomear pretended to be ill. In connivance with the king's sorcerer, she told the king that the girls had bewitched her with the "evil eye" and that she could not recover unless the girls' eyes were removed. Obsessed by his new wife, the king ordered his servants to cut out the eyes of the twelve girls; but the youngest one, **Neang Peou** had hidden, and since the king's men had not counted the girls, she was spared. The king sent them away to live in a cavern, unaware that they all were pregnant. Santhomear collected the eyes, put them in a silver bowl, and sent it to her daughter's palace.

Each girl gave birth to a child who was dead. However, the youngest and most intelligent girl, Neang Peou, gave birth to a beautiful boy whom she named **RithiSen**. Neang Peou managed to raise her son until he was old enough to go out and look for food for them. She told her sisters that he was an orphan. Young RithiSen went outside the cavern and played with other children. He was so clever that he made enough money to buy himself a rooster, and engaged in cockfights in which his rooster almost always won. With his winnings, he bought food, clothes, and other necessities to make life in the cave more comfortable for his mother and aunts. RithiSen grew up to be a very handsome young man. His reputation, as a clever and good-looking young man, reached Queen Santhomear, who had him followed to the cave. When she discovered that RithiSen was indeed Neang Peou's son, she immediately set out to destroy him, to prevent him from taking over the throne in the future. She called her best servant and confidant and said: "My good friend, go to the stable, arm yourself with the fastest horse, and take this sealed envelope to RithiSen. Tell him to hand carry the envelope to my daughter, Neang Kang Rei, at my other kingdom."

The letter was written as follows: "To my daughter: if RithiSen arrives at night, kill him at night. If he arrives in the day time, kill him in the day time."

The dispatcher had no difficulty in finding RithiSen, who obediently took the letter and the horse. He then bade goodbye to his mother and aunts and began his journey, without knowing that he was carrying his own death sentence.

The travel was long, treacherous, and eventful. One day, feeling completely exhausted, he made himself comfortable under a big tree and fell soundly asleep. In the meantime, Preah Entrea, foreseeing Santhomear's cruel purpose, sent a hermit to save RithiSen's life. The hermit walked to the tree, opened the pouch containing the deadly message, tore it up into pieces, and wrote a new one saying: "When RithiSen arrives, marry him at once." Having done that, the hermit sealed the letter, put it back in the pouch under the horse's neck, and left.

RithiSen woke up, refreshed. Joyfully, he continued his journey in search of Neang Kang Rei. He finally arrived at her kingdom and asked to present the letter to her. After having read the content of the letter, Neang Kang Rei was full of joy and ordered her ministers, servants, and the whole population to celebrate this happy occasion with all the pomp and magnificence it deserved.

After the festivities, Neang Kang Rei proceeded to show her husband her kingdom, her palace, and her people. One day, when they arrived at a small house within the palace, she hesitated.

Noticing her hesitation, RithiSen asked: "Dear wife, why are your hands trembling? What is there in this house?"

To which Neang Kang Rei replied: "Beloved husband, in this house there is a silver bowl containing the eyes of the twelve wives of my stepfather, Preah Bat Roth Sothi. In the same bowl, there is a small bottle that contains a potion that can restore sight to the eyes when they are returned to the faces of the women. There is also a magic wand that can create mountains, seas, or whatever you desire."

RithiSen was deeply saddened by this news, but tried to hide his emotions from his wife. At supper, he ordered a sumptuous meal with wine, music, and dancing. They ate and drank until they were exhausted. At midnight, after having made sure that his wife was sleeping soundly, he stole the keys to the secret house, opened it, and took the silver bowl, the potion and the wand. He quickly returned to the palace, kissed his wife lightly on the forehead, whispered a soft goodbye to her, and left. On his long journey, he met a hermit (the same one sent by Preah Entrea previously).

The hermit said: "My dear son, take this branch with you and keep going forward. If your wife catches up with you, just drop this branch. It will create a river between you and her. Go on, my child."

RithiSen was very grateful for the old man's advice and the precious gift. Without delay, he mounted his horse and continued his journey toward his father's kingdom. He was many hundreds of miles away when Neang Kang Rei woke up and noticed the disappearance of her husband. She called all her ministers, confidants, and servants and set forth in search of RithiSen. After several days, she caught up with him and begged him to come back. Ignoring his own sadness at the sight of his wife's distress, RithiSen regretfully dropped the branch on the ground. (This place is now known as **Kompong Léng** – Dropping River.) Suddenly, waters rushed from every direction, creating a big river separating him from his wife. Neang Kang Rei called her husband in vain from the other bank (this place is called **Kompong Hao** – Calling River). Tears poured down her cheeks when she realized that he would not return to her. She told her ministers, servants, and confidants to go back to the palace. In despair, she lay down on the bank of the river and died. Legend said that the spot where she died raised two mountains, representing the breasts of Neang Kang Rei – whereby the name of Mountain Kang Rei.

Fighting his sorrow, RithiSen waved his magic wand, which carried him high in the air with his horse, toward his father's kingdom. When he arrived, he denounced Queen Santhomear's cruelty. The latter was later killed by the king's men. He ordered his mother and his aunts be brought back to the palace, where he restored their sight and their former status as the King's wives.

After having done all that, he bid goodbye to his father, mother, aunts, and left to become a Buddhist priest. It was believed that RithiSen was Buddha's reincarnation.

THE POND OF THE
HIDDEN PLOUGH
Trapang Lak Neangkal

In the province of Kompong Chhnang, there is a famous pond called **Trapang Lak NeangKal**, or the Pond of the Hidden Plough. The name came from the following story:

In the village of **Rolear Phaear**, there lived an orphan. Nobody knew what had happened to his parents and grandparents, or whether he had any brothers or sisters. He had no known relatives in the neighborhood. In Cambodia, orphans usually seek refuge at the temple, where the monks teach them to read and write.

This orphan found himself a sponsor, an old monk at the temple called **Bay Mauk**. As he seemed to be an honest boy, the old monk took pity on him, gave him shelter, and tried to teach him, but the boy showed no progress in his learning. He was unable to go beyond the eleventh letter of the Khmer alphabet. If a new lesson was thrust upon him, he forgot the old one. Every day he tried to recite the alphabet **Nor Mo** up to the letter **Ik Ey**. But there his memory failed him. In arithmetic, he was at a total loss. He could neither add nor subtract. All day, he kept reciting **Ik Ei, Ik Ei** in a loud voice, to such an extent that he became known as **Chau Ik Ei** or Ik Ei Boy. Many years passed.

The old monk, his master, was very discouraged by all his efforts for this orphan. He said to himself: "Chau Ik Ei cannot learn anything other than eleven letters of the alphabet. However, he has demonstrated a deep respect for elders; moreover, he is honest and loyal. I should not complain."

The monk then summoned Chau Ik Ei and said: "Ik Ei Boy, you came to me at an early age; now you have become a grown up young man. I have tried everything I could to teach you all these years, but to no avail. You seem to have a limited capacity to absorb reading and writing. But you possess other qualities such as the ability to listen to people and to take orders graciously. You are also loyal and you have learned the virtue of respect for your elders."

He then thought for a moment and continued: "But you cannot live and depend on me for the rest of your life. I am going to introduce you to a friend of mine, a high government official. The king has high esteem for this man. He may be able to find you a job."

Ik Ei listened to his master obediently and said: "Lok Ta (Grandfather), I will be very pleased to do whatever you want me to do. I know that you are very concerned about my well-being and my future. You have always been good to me and looked after my interests with a kind heart."

After Ik Ei had packed his few belongings, he and the monk left the temple for the government official's home in the city. When they arrived, the old monk introduced Ik Ei to his friend.

"Honorable friend, I have brought you this very capable young man to serve you and your family. Please give him a chance. Teach him as much as you can. He is very loyal, honest, and eager to learn new skills. If by mistake he misinterprets your orders and tasks, please forgive him. For all the years that I have watched him grow under my roof, I can assure you that he never makes a mistake intentionally."

The government official thanked the old monk for bringing

such an honest young man to serve him and his family. Years passed. Ik Ei lived and served his new master and family devotedly. His conduct was beyond reproach. However, his new master also realized that Ik Ei had a very limited capability for learning. He was still unable to read or write. This handicap had prevented him from finding a better job in the government.

Realizing that he could not find a good job, Ik Ei decided to leave his new family and go back to the temple to become a monk. He bade goodbye to his master and his family and went back to the village where he used to live. Because he lacked learning skills, he was ordained only to the lowest rank of the priesthood. In his old age he became known as "Lok Ta Ik Ei" or "Grandfather Ik Ei."

The Buddhist community provides materials such as Buddhist robes, sandals, tea, sugar, incense sticks, candles -- all materials needed for the strict observance of Buddhist rites. Well-known monks are usually inundated with gifts of various kinds from their followers, as well as an abundant food supply all year round. In general, each monk takes a student called **Kaun Seus** (young student) under his protection. The student takes care of the monk's property and daily maintenance tasks, such as cleaning, cooking, and distributing excess supplies to the poor in the village, if any. In return the monk teaches the student how to read and write and other skills necessary for him to get a job in the community or in the government.

Because of his reputation as an illiterate monk, Lok Ta Ik Ei could not find a student, or Kaun Seus, to serve him. Food was scarce even for his once-a-day meal as required by Buddhist tradition. Finally, a boy named **Chau Yauk**, or "young Yauk," took pity on the monk and offered to be his Kaun Seus. In November there is a national memorial day for all Buddhists. On that day, the entire village celebrates. Farmers, their families, and inhabitants of the nearby village flock to the temple to offer prayers and food in remembrance of deceased parents, brothers and sisters, children, and all other loved ones who have passed away. **Nuum Ansaum** (cakes made of sticky rice with yellow beans and pork, or bananas) and cooked in banana-leaf wrappings were served as the main dishes for that occasion. That year, the harvest was plentiful, and generous offerings were displayed at the monk's hut called **Kod** during the three-day celebration, except at the hut of Lok Ta Ik Ei. He received hardly anything.

Chau Yauk had a brilliant idea. At night, he went from kod to kod (from hut to hut) collecting Nuum Ansaum wrappings and piling them up under his master's hut to make people believe that Lok Ta Ik Ei had received the most offerings in the temple during the festivities.

The rainy season arrived. Farmers were busy getting their paddy fields ready for sowing. They left their houses early in the morning to plough the fields and did not return home until sundown. One day, Chau Yauk, wandering around near a pond at sunset, saw a farmer unhook his plough (called **Neangkal**) from his oxen, and called it a day by taking his oxen home. The farmer left the plough near the pond. Suddenly, Chau Yauk had an idea. After the farmer's departure, he took the plough apart and hid each piece in different places of the pond. Then he went back to his hut and related the event to Lok Ta Ik Ei.

"Lok Ta, I took a farmer's plough apart and hid it in the pond," he said. "The handle is hidden in the south corner of the pond, its blade in the east near Doeum Ampil (tamarind tree). Please take note of these facts."

The next day, Chau Yauk went back to the pond to observe the farmer. He found the latter very upset.

"**AVar Oeuy**," (a nickname given to a young child, similar

to "Hi, boy"), the farmer said to Chau Yauk, "I lost my plough. Somebody stole it last night. I left it right here, this very spot. Have you seen it? I do not know what to do; I need my plough to finish my work to get my fields ready for the seeds. I do not have money to buy a new one."

To that, Chau Yauk replied: "Please don't be sad, **Pou** [uncle]. Take some offerings to my master, Lok Ta Ik Ei. He can make accurate predictions. He will help you find your plough."

Having said that, he ran as fast as he could back to the temple.

"Lok Ta, the farmer is coming shortly to ask you where he can find the plough," he yelled to Lok Ta Ik Ei. "Remember what I told you last night. Please tell him exactly what I said." Then he sat in a corner and waited.

In the meantime, the farmer went back home and told his wife to prepare offerings such as food, tea, sugar, betel nuts, incense sticks, and candles. Without delay, he pressed forward to Lok Ta Ik

Ei's hut. When he saw the monk, he prostrated himself three times before him.

"Why do you look distressed, my good man?" the old monk asked. The farmer replied: "Please accept these offerings. I have heard that you can make good predictions. Somebody stole my plough last night. As you know, I need it to finish the fields before the rainy season ends. If I can have my four acres ready, I can expect a generous harvest next spring. I cannot afford to buy a new plough."

Lok Ta Ik Ei pretended to make some calculations on a piece of paper and said:

"Your plough was stolen indeed. But go back to the pond near your rice fields, and you'll find it. However, it was taken apart. You can find the handle hidden in the south corner of the pond, and the blade in the east corner near the tamarind tree."

The farmer was very excited and happy upon hearing the good news. He prostrated himself three times before the monk, whispered his profound gratitude, and promised to bring more offerings if the plough was found. He then hurried back to the pond. He went to the exact spots indicated by the monk and found every piece of the plough.

From that day forward, Lok Ta Ik Ei became well known as a fortune teller. To this day, the pond is named **Trapang Lak NeangKal**, which means Pond of the Hidden Plough.

MALE AND FEMALE MOUNTAINS
Phnom Pros Phnom Srey

Along the great Mekong River lies the province of Kompong Cham, one of the richest provinces of Cambodia. All provinces established along the river begin heir names with **Kompong**, meaning "riverbank." One can reach Kompong Cham by boat or via the National Route 7 from Cambodia's capital city, Phnom Penh. At exactly 116 Km from Phnom Penh, on the west side of route 7, and 1 km into the countryside, one can see two man-made mountains side by side. They are named **Phnom Pros** and **Phnom Srey**. (Phnom meaning mountain, Pros meaning man, and Srey meaning woman).

The story is as follows:

Once upon a time, Cambodia (or Kampuchea, as it is sometimes called) was ruled by an unmarried Queen named **Srey Ayuthya**. Because of her high position, nobody dared ask to marry her. Feeling lonely and desiring children, she decreed that all women must look for suitable husbands and propose to them, which was contrary to the traditional way of having men propose to women. Thereafter, under Queen Ayuthya's reign, all women had the right to seek intelligent, good-looking young men of good fortune whom they thought would make good husbands and fathers for their children.

However, this law had a flaw. It did not work for all women. Some intelligent women, who possessed neither fortune nor good looks, were rejected when they proposed. The young men chose only those women with such superficial qualities.

After Queen Ayuthya died, the women decided to change that law to one that would prevent the rejection of unfortunate women. They thought the law under Queen Ayuthya was not only unfair to all women, but it was also degrading to have women proposing to men. The women then formed a committee and came up with a plan to change that law. They asked that young eligible men also form a committee. The plan was to ask both committees with the same number of members to compete in building two mountains. Whoever would build the highest mountain would win, and the losing team would propose marriage. Each committee had to commence building its mountain at dusk and finish at dawn when the morning star rose.

Both committees agreed. Each side recruited the agreed number of eligible bachelors. At the moment scheduled for the competition, they began their work. After several hours of hard work, the women's committee came up with another plan. Since young men were physically stronger than women and could therefore win the competition, they decided on a stratagem. Around midnight they planted a very tall pole near the young men's newly built mountain and hoisted a lamp at the top of the pole.

The young men's committee, seeing the light and thinking it was the morning star, stopped their work and went to sleep. In the meantime, all the young women continued their endeavors until the actual rise of the morning star.

Finally, when the roosters began crowing their morning

"Cock-a-doodle-doo" all the young men realized that they had been duped by the women's committee. But it was too late. The women's mountain was then higher than theirs, and the men agreed thenceforth to propose marriage to women for all time.

THE STORY OF BATTAMBANG

This story came to me courtesy of Mr. William N. Harben, a retired U.S. diplomat posted in Phnom Penh, Cambodia in 1970.

Each province of Cambodia is rich in legends like this one, unique to its name and culture. The **Battambang** province is located in the northern part of Phnom Penh, close to the border of Thailand. It is the second richest province of Cambodia. The name Battambang means "Lost Stick."

Children like to listen to stories. One evening a group of them went to an old man who used to sit and watch them play under a tree. They said to him: "Sir, this town is called "Lost Stick" in our language. How could a town come to have such a name?"

The old man smiled and told them all to sit down and listen, for it was a long story.

Once upon a time, a farmer, while looking for firewood in a deep forest, found a very rare and valuable ebony tree. But this tree was somewhat different from other black trees. One of the branches was sticking out as if waiting to be cut. The farmer, entranced by this particular branch, decided to cut it as a souvenir. Back at home, he polished the branch, gave it a shape, and made a walking stick out of it which in his family was called simply "the ebony stick" – **Dambang Kranhoung** in Cambodian. The stick was kept among his most precious possessions and he used it sparingly. The farmer soon discovered that his black stick had magical powers, because it seemed to give the farmer some mysterious persona. Everything seemed to be in his favor. He found himself surrounded by people of all ranks, rich and poor, young and old, men and women who voted him as their leader. His popularity among the surrounding population was so great that he wanted to use it to his advantage. He mounted a big war against King **Chak Krapat** who ruled at the great city of **Angkor Wat** at the time, overthrew him and bestowed upon himself the title of **Preah Bat Dambang** Kranhoung or "Ebony Stick King," for he believed that the stick had brought him victory.

He ruled for seven years, seven months, and seven days. On the last day, he saw a very bright star from the terrace of his vast palace. He was very puzzled by its appearance. He summoned his astrologers and asked them what the star portended. The astrologers, using all their skills to detect any unusual movement in their astrological charts that might influence a particular event on earth, told the king that somewhere in the kingdom a child was about to be born. They warned the king that this child would later seize power from him and dethrone him. Having heard that, the king went into a rage and ordered his soldiers to kill all women who were going to become mothers in the kingdom, and to burn their bodies afterwards.

In a remote village far away, a soldier had just killed a young woman and hauled her body to the big fire to be burned. In doing so, a baby boy was dropped from the dead mother onto the fire. The boy's legs and arms were burnt. By a miracle, he survived and was swiftly picked up by a farmer who put him in a rattan basket and took him to a distant pagoda, a Buddhist temple. The boy was then raised by Buddhist monks who named him **Prohm** and taught him to read, write, and to be a good citizen. However, his childhood injuries left him crippled. Instead of walking, he was confined to slide on his bottom. For this, he was given the name of **Prohmkel** or "Prohm the Slider."

Many years went by. One night, at the palace, the king saw another bright star next to the moon, surrounded by three rings of different colors like a rainbow. The star was so bright that it overshadowed the moon. Perplexed by this new event, and unsure of his lasting power, he consulted his astrologers once more as to the meaning of this unusual star. The astrologers responded that a child with greater powers than his had already been born, and within seven days, a young man on a white horse would come from the northeast, seize power from him, and take over the throne.

The king was enraged to hear that anyone dared to come and challenge his supreme power. He gathered all his soldiers and took all precautions necessary to prepare for this undesirable intrusion.

Rumors of the arrival of a **Neak Mean Bun** (meaning a powerful leader sent from heaven) on a white horse spread throughout the country. People traveled from every corner of the kingdom to the city of Angkor Wat to witness the prospective leader's coming. Some came by boats, some came on horses, some came in oxcarts, and some walked.

The news also spread to the northeast part of the kingdom where Prohmkel lived. Prohm, in short, also expressed a desire to see the Neak Mean Bun. He went to the head monk and asked permission to go to Angkor Wat to behold the arrival of this heaven-sent leader. His request granted, he set out upon the road with the crowd, but since he could not walk, he fell far behind the stream of travelers. Exhausted, he stopped under a big tree for a short rest. Suddenly, an old hermit holding the reins of a white horse with his right hand appeared. His left hand carried a container of food. He also had a small bag of clothes on his back.

When he saw Prohm, he said: "Young man, will you please take care of my horse and my belongings while I attend to some urgent business in the forest?"

To that, Prohm replied: "Lok Ta, how can I take care of your things when both my arms are glued to my body and both my legs are also glued together?"

The hermit replied: "Don't worry. I will attach your hands to the horse with a rope. This way, the horse will not run away." He did so and disappeared into the forest.

The horse was strikingly beautiful. Prohm wished he could run his fingers along the horse's back, feel its smooth white shiny skin, its white tail and silky white mane. While Prohm was quietly admiring the horse, the horse took a few steps around him. Suddenly the horse jumped and whinnied. In doing so, he pulled both Prohm's arms apart. To his great surprise, no scars or deformation were seen on the new arms or the body.

Prohm thought aloud: "By pulling the rope attached to my arms, this horse was able to return my arms to normal; therefore, he may be able to do the same thing to my legs."

Having said that, he used his now free hands to attach his legs to the horse, and waited. The horse looked at the rope for a while and gently pulled it. Prohm's legs were freed from his injuries and returned to normal. Prohm was very surprised to see this new transformation of his body. He not only could use his arms, move his legs, and walk like a normal human being, but it seemed he had become a handsome one as well.

Patiently, he waited for the hermit, the owner of the horse, to return. Hours went by. There was no sign of him. Prohm was getting hungry. Unable to still his hunger and thirst by looking at the food container sitting near him, he opened it. What he saw and smelled was beyond his expectations. It smelled delightfully delicious and made his mouth water. Too much temptation! He ate the food, which he thought must have come from the gods, washed it down with the heavenly-smelling water, and proceeded to open the bag. He took out the clothes inside and got dressed. Everything fit as if the clothes had been tailored for him. He approached the horse and decided to take him for a short ride. As soon as he mounted the horse, it immediately fled at lightning speed, taking its new master to the royal palace several hundred miles away.

The horse stopped in the area not far from the town of Angkor Thom, where King Dambang Kranhoung resided. The king, enraged to see such an arrogant intruder in the vicinity of his palace, went to his throne where he hid his magic stick in a silver holder, picked it up, and threw it at the young man. The stick missed its target, flew hundreds of miles away and fell in a forest which then came to be known as "Forest of the Lost Stick" or in Khmer **Bat Dambang**. ("Bat" meaning "Lost," and "Dambang" meaning "Stick"). Later, the spelling was changed to Battambang. Today, Battambang, with its proximity to **Siemreap**, has become the second richest province in Cambodia.

Sensing that he was powerless without his magic stick, King Dambang Kranhoung entered a secret passage, left the palace, and fled to safety in Thailand.

A cheerful crowd rushed from everywhere to see the young man draped in royal clothing standing by the white horse, and they knew that he was the new Neak Mean Bun sent from above to rule the kingdom. They escorted him to the palace and declared him the new king under the name of **Preah Bat** Prohmkel, or King Prohmkel. Later, the king was also known as **Preah Bat Santhop Aknureach**. To pay tribute to the horse that helped him to power, Preah Bat Prohmkel ordered a flag, in the middle of which stood a white horse. The white horse flag became the national symbol during his reign.

At another village named **Samroung Chong Kal** in the province of Siemreap, where Prohmkel had received the horse from the hermit, a temple **(Prasat)** about 5.5 meters high and 15 to 16 meters in diameter, was built in his honor. Inside, in the center, there is a throne, or **Palaing**. This temple is flanked by 2 man-made lakes on the east and west. Farther north, approximately 150 meters from the temple, there is a river.

THE STORY OF PROHM BACHEY
Vat Nokor BaChey

If one travels on route 7 from Phnom Penh to the province of Kompong Cham, at approximately three kilometers from the city, there is a service road on the left leading to the remaining gates of an old monument built of brown sandstone. The gates were broken, torn by time and neglect, possibly by many wars that took place over the centuries. This monument is called **Vat Nokor BaChey** or **Vat Nokor** or **Temple BaChey**. Once inside the compound, you would find two more sets of broken gates made of the same sandstone, all having entrances facing North, South, East and West. In the middle of the inner gates, a big platform of 15 meters by 15 meters was erected in the form a **stupa** (a sacred Buddhist construction that used to hold ashes of deceased parents, relatives and other family members). It has four open doors, in the middle of each of them stood a stone Buddha serenely facing the four directions.

At the outer gates, between the entrance three and four, one or two small Buddhist temples were also built. On the south side, one of the temples had also housed four small buddhas, also facing the four directions.

The story goes like this:

Once upon a time, a powerful king called **Sdach Krahn** (King Krahn) was searching for a place to settle and build his palace. On his long journey, escorted by his high ranking administrators, his many concubines, his retinue, his soldiers and his servants, he came upon a small river that flowed into the big one (which became the Mekong River later) in the province of Kompong Cham. He ordered his people to erect camps there for more exploration. The river was full of fish of all kinds. At the monsoon season, the overflowing Mekong River spread its bounty to the smaller rivers, which overflowed and created good soil for the people who lived off the river. The fertilized banks became the farmland for growing all kinds of edible vegetables and fruit. Everything seemed to grow wild. During the harvest season, people from as far as five miles around gathered in their multi-colored clothing to harvest the fruit of their labor, or to barter their produce for food they didn't have. The annual harvest season was also the time when young men and young women met one another, flirted with one another, and made their matrimonial choices. There were games, songs, and dancing everywhere, from sunrise to sundown. Further away, inside the city, there were also plenty of valuable trees such as Teak, Koki, and Kranhoung (a black precious tree), to cut and use for building a city. The perfect weather all year round also added to the desirability of the area.

The king decided to make this place his kingdom. However, the river belonged to a very nice young woman named **Neang Peou**, who made her living from the fish she and her people caught from that river. Upon learning that a king had arrived and decided to stay, she instructed her one hundred and two servants to prepare plenty of food and abundant desserts, and to pick different kinds of fruit from her orchards as offerings to the king. The next day, a procession of beautiful girls in their most colorful silk clothing and jewelry carried silver trays full of flowers, food, and fruit through the pathways to the king's camps. These girls, all dressed up in white embroidered silk skirts called **sampots**, their arms and ankles encased in glittering gold and silver ornaments, looked like **Asparas** – celestial angels from heaven.

The procession was headed by Neang Peou. She herself carried a special silver tray of white lilies for the king. At the entrance to the camps, she was greeted by the king's guards and high ranking officials, who took her straight to the king's quarters. The king was very pleased to see that he and his people were so handsomely welcomed to this area. Not only was he impressed by her generosity, but also by her beauty, her gracefulness, and her youth. Her radiant smile, her long wavy black hair coming down to the waist, and her young firm body molded by a red silk sampot, had instantly captured his heart. After the offerings ceremony, Neang Peou bowed before the king and bid him goodbye, to return to her house. To her delight, the king promised to see more of her in the coming days.

From then on, every day the king and a small group of his entourage went to visit Neang Peou. Sometimes he stayed for dinner at her request. Their relationship flourished. As the days went by, he fell more and more in love with Neang Peou, and through a go-between, he asked her to marry him. They were married soon after with pomp and fanfare, attended by many other kings and their queens, their soldiers and their servants from neighboring provinces. The celebration lasted a week, with all kinds of activities. Food and drink were plentiful for everyone. After the festivities had died down, the king, who was so much in love with his new wife, ordered a monument protected by three layers of gates in pink sandstone to be built in her honor.

Two years later, the culmination of their happiness was fulfilled by the arrival of a boy. The king's happiness knew no bounds.

He showered his son with gifts, toys, and best of all, with love. The young prince grew up in a household full of games, and with affection from both parents. He was full of perk and energy, and possessed a good sense of curiosity for a boy his age. In brief, he was a very intelligent young boy, questioning everything that came his way.

The king said to himself: "My son is very smart. I have to find him good tutors for higher education."

In the old days, the only place to get a good education was in the faraway country of China. So, when the young prince reached the age of eight years old, the king and Neang Peou decided that he should go to China for a formal education. With a heavy heart, he ordered his soldiers to build a boat that could carry a number of servants, soldiers, his son, and an ample supply of food to last several months until his son reached China. The day came to say goodbye to his son. Both he and Neang Peou, tears running down their cheeks, held their son tight for a moment in their arms.

The king then said: "Son, go to China. Learn as much as you can, and bring that knowledge back to our homeland. Goodbye, my son!"

The young prince was a brave prince. Without shedding a tear, he promised his father he would come back and take over his reign. He did not know that he never would see his father again, as the latter died a few years later of sorrow and illness. The prince's mother, Neang Peou, left the palace and went back to her home near the river. A new king had moved the kingdom to another area of Kompong Cham, called **Bah Phhnom**.

In China, the young prince learned everything required to govern a kingdom, including military skills, philosophy, and astrology. His sharp intelligence had won the hearts of high ranking Chinese officials, who expressed their desire to keep him in China. They spread rumors that his parents had died, and that it would be pointless to go back. When the prince reached the age of eighteen, he was offered a prestigious position with the Chinese government.

While working for the Chinese, he never stopped studying. After meetings, he always went to the best academy library to learn more, to do more research on the specific details of any particular project. His skills in the military field, his outlook in philosophy, and his acute sense in astrology had gained him the Chinese name of **Sampav Kong**, or the man of great three skills (Sam means three). His reputation had spread throughout China. He was well liked, admired, and respected by all the Chinese. One day, he went to the Emperor and asked permission to spend time in the countryside with the people so he could learn more about them, about their needs, their aspirations, and what the government could do to improve their lives. Permission granted, he embarked on his long journey for the truth. He declined all offers of escort, and did not accept any money for expenditures during the trip. Instead, he disguised himself as an ordinary peasant, wearing peasant clothes, just to be one of them. He moved from place to place, collecting information for his studies, making a simple living as a fortune teller. He did so well that people flocked from everywhere to get their fortune told and paid him generously. His humble disguise had gained him even more respect throughout China.

However, the prince, now aged thirty, longed to go back to his homeland and to see through his own eyes what his people looked like and what they did, although he did not remember much of his childhood. Again his disguise as a peasant helped him roam around the countryside without being recognized, and to escape from China. For seven months, he stayed in different places. When he arrived inside Cambodia, he took refuge in a temple where he could learn Cambodian or Khmer, his own language. With zeal and dedication, he was able to speak and read Khmer fluently in record time. He adopted a new name, **Prohm**. Now that he had grasped the language, he left the temple and moved further inside the country, looking for the place where he was born, Kompong Cham.

He arrived at a village and saw an old house at the outskirts of the city. Exhausted from his long journey, he knocked at the door of the old house to see whether he could find a place to rest for the night until the next day. He was pleasantly greeted by a lady of approximately fifty years of age. She looked very beautiful, her skin was smooth, and she had no wrinkles. Her manner showed that she was an upper-class lady. She had a soft voice, and when she invited him in, his heart was pounding with excitement. She ordered her servants to prepare him a room and to offer him some food before he retired for the night after such a long day. The next day, Prohm thanked the lady of the house profusely and stated that he was very delighted to be so welcome. The lady told him she had some business to carry out, and she needed a man to help. If he had no other plans in the near future, he was very welcome to stay free of charge. Prohm was overjoyed by the offer and accepted. They lived together as business partners for a while. She taught him business skills he didn't have. Prohm, however, was more and more attracted to the lady in spite of their age difference. She possessed all virtues of a woman he was looking for as a wife: compassion for the poor, honesty, generosity and, most of all, her gentleness towards him.

As time went by, he made new friends. One day, with help from one of his new friends, he asked for her hand in marriage. As mentioned before, the lady had lost all relatives and lived only with a handful of faithful and loyal servants. She was also attracted to Prohm. She accepted his proposal and shortly thereafter they were married. They were a happily married couple, well liked and respected by everyone in the neighborhood.

One day, the memory of her eight-year old son came back. She felt sad and knowing her husband had accurate skills for telling fortunes, she asked him to look at the zodiac sign to see what had happened to the son she had sent to China some thirty years ago. Prohm, intrigued by the question, asked her what year she had sent her son and what her husband was doing at the time. She revealed that her husband had been King Sdach Krahn of this province, and she had been his wife. They had a beautiful son, so smart they decided to send him to China for higher education in order to come back and govern the country. She revealed that her husband died a few years later of illness and sadness at the loss of the son they sent away.

She added: "Look at this river by our house, that's where my husband the king and I used to canoe in the evening as a pastime. We named it **Tonlé Om** – The Cruiser River." (The name exists to this day.)

To her astonishment, she saw Prohm prostrated in front of her both his hands joined together, tears running down his cheeks. Sadly, he said: "Dear venerable mother, I am the one you sent to China when I was eight years old. I never, for one moment in my life, thought my mother was still alive, and never in my wildest dreams imagined that one day I would become her husband. I beg your forgiveness for my sins. Please tell me what I should do to be relieved of this shameful sin. I will do anything."

The old lady was shocked, astounded, stunned by these words. She herself never thought she would ever see her son again and least of all marry him. Tears ran down her cheeks. She remained speechless for a long moment. It seemed like an eternity. Finally, sobbing uncontrollably, she said: "Oh my beloved son, what karma has drawn us together in this sinful way? I am as embarrassed as you are. Here is what I think you should do. When I die, you must bury me in a stupa located at the old palace of **Nokor Bachey**, which your father had built for me. My coffin must be surrounded by four stone buddhas standing at each corner of the coffin. Then when you die, you must make it known that a stone copy of you in a sitting position on a small platform with your hands joined together must be placed in front of my coffin facing the west asking forgiveness until the end of the Buddhist calendar year. Only in this way can you be relieved of your sins."

Prohm bowed his head to his mother and promised he would fulfill her every wish when the time came.

They continued to live together, this time as mother and son. A few years later, the old lady died. Fulfilling his promise, Prohm had a stupa built under which he buried his mother, surrounded by four sandstone buddhas. Later, the people in the community built a temple over the stupa to protect it from the weather.

When Prohm, in turn, died, his students built a sandstone copy of him, with his hands joined and facing his mother's stupa to the west.

In China, when Prohm or "Sampav Kong" disappeared without any trace for several years, the Chinese government sent their investigators to look for him. Unfortunately, when they arrived in Kampuchea (the old name for Cambodia), Prohm had just died. In recognition of his great work for China, the Chinese officials ordered that his Chinese name, Sampav Kong, be inscribed in the stone. This monument, along with others built in Bachey, became a tourist attraction in the years to come. Every year, during the Chinese New Year and during the memorial month of November, people flocked to the temple to pay their respects to Prohm, or Sampav Kong. In the Buddhist year of 2070, it was believed that some businessmen tried to move the stone and placed it at the entrance of the gate. Consequently, it was said that the whole area was stricken by a mysterious disease during which time several hundreds died. The legend went to say that Prohm's ghost came to the house of an old lady and told her to move his statue back to the original place. He told her he had to face his mother's coffin for her forgiveness until the end of the Buddhist calendar year. And so they did, and everything went back to normal.

THE CROCODILE NEN THON
Krapoeu Nen Thon

This story originated at **Sambor**, a small village in the province of **Kratié** on the Mekong river.

It was told that a young Buddhist monk named **Thon** raised a crocodile as a pet. For newly ordained monks, the designation of **Nen** is affixed to his first name to indicate he is still a novice. Thus, he was called Nen Thon. Later the crocodile became known as "Crocodile Nen Thon" or **Krapoeu Nen Thon** (Krapeu means crocodile in Cambodian language). The monk was very fond of his pet. Every evening, at sunset, he went to the river bank to talk and play with the crocodile. They both enjoyed seeing each other. People who lived in the nearby villages, men, women, children, monks of all ages used to come to the river for a swim and watch the master and his pet without fear, because the monk had power over his pet. Every evening, the monk firmly reminded the crocodile not to harm anyone. The monk also possessed healing powers; as such, he was well respected, well liked, and sought after to restore health to sick people. His reputation spread beyond his hometown.

At that time, the capital of Cambodia or Kampuchea was located at **Oudong** on the **Bassac** river. The king who had established his fortress in that town had a lovely young daughter.

Suddenly, the princess contracted a mysterious disease and became very ill. Alarmed by this grave illness, he ordered his staff to find the best doctor in the kingdom to cure her. He had heard of Nen Thon's reputation as a healer. He immediately sent for him. In those days, people traveled by small boats. It took several days to travel from Kratié to Oudong and the trip was treacherous and fraught with dangers. Between Kratié and the village of **Chhlong** on the Mekong river, there were other fearful crocodiles, cataracts, and sharp rocks which could easily sink small boats and drown their passengers. Even so, the monk arrived safely at the King's palace. He immediately began to apply his healing powers to the little princess. After a few weeks, the princess regained her strength and energy, and her good health had returned. However, fearful that his daughter's illness would recur, the king ordered the monk to stay longer.

At Kratié, the crocodile very much missed his master whom he had not seen for several months. Every evening he went to the same spot to look for any sign of his master's return. Full of sadness, he decided to go to Oudong to fetch his beloved monk. Upon his arrival at a place near Chhlong called **Phnom Soparkaly** or Mount Soparkaly, he encountered a fierce enemy, a nasty counterpart. The latter, thinking that crocodile Nen Thon was intruding in this territory, was ready to attack and destroy him. Crocodile Nen Thon, on the other hand, although bigger, and more powerful, was in no mood for fighting. He was in a hurry to find his master. Wisely, he avoided the fight, but promised to himself that he would come back one day and deal with this impudent enemy.

When he arrived at Oudong, he hid himself from the inhabitants living along the river in deep waters. He knew that they would not understand the friendship between a crocodile and a monk. They would certainly be frightened and outraged to see such a large crocodile in the neighborhood. He kept hoping that one day, his master would come to the bank of the river to bathe or admire the sunset. Sure enough, one evening, the monk came by and sat upon a bamboo raft. Seeing his master, he lifted himself to the surface of the water and swam toward him. The monk delightedly recognized his pet at once. However, without warning, crocodile Nen Thon quickly decided to take his master home. He smashed the raft with his tail, slid himself under his master, and carried him on his back toward his hometown.

After a few days of travel, both Crocodile Nen Thon and the monk arrived at the same spot where the crocodile's enemy lived. **Athon** (this was the crocodile's nickname) thought to himself: *"This crocodile is looking for a fight. But he does not know I am stronger and more powerful than him. He does not know that whoever wants to fight with me must*

perish. Well, I am going to teach him a lesson." Then he had a second thought: *"If I fight him, my master will be in danger. He would be thrown off my back and drown or eaten by my enemy. I must save my master. And the only way to do that is to hide him in my stomach."*

Having said that, Crocodile Nen Thon swallowed his master whole and attacked his fierce enemy in full force. The fight lasted several hours. Finally the battle was over. Having successfully killed his opponent, he continued his journey toward Sambor, where he intended to spit up his master as soon as he landed. At his arrival, young children, monks and people living near the temple gathered to cheer him. They were happy to see him back and were hoping to see the monk also. Athon crawled to the sand on the bank of the river and spat up his master. Alas, to his deep sorrow, his master had died several hours ago.

The people shouted at him: "What a horrible animal you are! You killed our beloved monk!"

Full of regret and sadness, Crocodile Nen Thon moved back into deep waters looking for a place to mourn his master and abate his sorrow. He was very sorry that he had to swallow his master, thus causing his death. He wished he could do something to bring the monk back to life. He said to himself: *"I love my master very much. I did not intend to harm him. If he died, it was not entirely my fault. The cause of my master's death was the king's daughter. Had she not been ill, my master would not have been called to cure her illness. Therefore, she must be punished."*

He then disappeared in deep waters again and swam toward Oudong with every intention to avenge his master's death. When he arrived, he waited near the bank of the river for the opportunity to seize the princess should she come to take a bath. The story did not say how long he had to wait. But one day, the princess indeed went to the river with her retinue and maids. While she was enjoying herself with her entourage in the water, Krapeu Nen Thon seized her, swallowed her, and left the area immediately. Needless to say, the king was devastated at this sad news! He ordered all his staff to pursue the crocodile and capture him at all costs. It was believed that he brought with him a seer (a fortune teller) who could tell the exact whereabouts of the crocodile.

Krapeu Nen Thon swam all the way to the Laotian border, near a place called the Khone Falls, and back to Kratié. Seeing he was intensively searched for in this area, he continued his travel looking for a safer place to hide. He swam through **Prek Chhlong**, a tributary of the Mekong river. Unfortunately, it was there that he was captured and split open to retrieve the princess. Like the monk, alas, the princess was long dead. Her body was brought back to Sambor for a royal cremation. The Crocodile Nen Thon was cut into pieces and his meat was salted and dried for food consumption. The story said this place was called **Veal Hal Ngiet** the "plain to dry meat."

THE STORY OF THMENH CHEY
(He Always Had The Last Word)

O nce upon a time, in the kingdom of **Tep Borey**, there was a woman about to give birth to her first child. In the wee hours of the morning, she had a strange dream. It was believed that any dreams that occurred in the early hours of the morning were the most accurate. She dreamed that she had picked all the coconuts from the coconut tree in her backyard. Then she saw the brightest star shining down on her face, which woke her up. Not sure what to make of this dream, she dressed quickly and went straight to a fortune teller living not very far from her house. The fortune teller listened attentively to the woman's description of her dream. Her chart showed that the woman would give birth to a boy with a great destiny. Instead of telling the truth, the fortune teller told her she would have a baby boy who would become a slave.

"You will have a boy who will later become a slave," she said.

Saddened, the woman went home. A few days later, she gave birth to a little boy whom she named **Thmenh Chey**. She raised her son lovingly, despite the fortune teller's prediction. The boy grew up normally, like other children, in a loving environment. He always went outside to play with other children, sometimes by himself under the house of a rich merchant. (Cambodian houses were built on stilts in those days.) One day, when he was eight years old, the lady of the house, while weaving, dropped her spool to the ground. Seeing Thmenh Chey playing down below, she called out:

"Son, would you please pick up my spool and bring it to me?"

"What are you going to give me if I pick up your spool?" he asked.

"I'll give you sweet rice cakes," she answered.

"How many?"

"Many!" she yelled back.

"All right, I'll bring it to you then," he said.

Thmenh Chey picked up the spool, climbed the stairs to the house, handed it to her, and moved away to sit in a corner awaiting his reward. The lady had her servants bring a basket of sweet rice cakes for Thmenh Chey. But he was not satisfied with the number he received.

"That's not enough," he said.

The merchant's wife ordered her maids to bring some more. Thmenh Chey still wanted a lot more. The lady told him that it was enough, that she would not give him any more. He began to cry.

"What is all this commotion about?" her husband inquired.

The lady explained to her husband that Thmenh Chey was very greedy and wanted more cakes.

To which he said: "Let me take care of the boy."

Having said that, the merchant ordered the maid to bring him a big flat bamboo basket. He took three cakes from the other basket and put them side by side in the new empty basket.

Turning to Thmenh Chey, he said: "Which basket do you want, son?"

"I want this new basket," the boy said hastily.

The merchant was happy to hand him the basket and get rid of the boy. On the way home, Thmenh Chey realized that he had been tricked by the merchant. He made up his mind to get his revenge. When he arrived back home, he gave the cakes to his mother and told her to go to the merchant's house and borrow money from him. As collateral for this debt, she must put him at the service of the merchant. His mother protested, saying that she would never sell her only son to be somebody else's servant. Thmenh Chey would not listen to her. He related the incident of the morning to his mother and told her this was the only way to get even with the merchant. After pleading with her son for several hours to no avail, she gave in.

Now Thmenh Chey worked for the merchant as part of the household staff. Every day, the merchant went to pay tribute to the king. Thmenh Chey's duty was to accompany him, carrying a betel nut box to the palace. The box contained four or five smaller boxes full of ingredients for the betel chew, which the Khmer people enjoyed since cigarettes were not yet known in Cambodia. The merchant, galloping on horseback, arrived at the palace far ahead of the boy. Thmenh Chey, on the contrary, had to run after the horse, carrying the big box that contained smaller boxes. Finally, he also arrived at the palace, out of breath.

"Why are you so late, boy?" the merchant inquired.

"Master, I could not run faster for fear of dropping all the small boxes on the way," he replied.

"From now on, I want you to arrive at the same time as I, regardless of the boxes," the merchant said.

The next day, Thmenh Chey put all the small boxes in the big one as usual, but deliberately did not close the lid. He ran after the merchant's horse as fast as his legs could carry him. In doing so, all the small boxes fell out along the way. The merchant went straight to the audience room, took his usual seat among other high ranking dignitaries, turned around, and asked Thmenh Chey to bring the betel nut box. The latter pushed the empty box toward his master, and crawled back to sit in a corner, awaiting further instructions. Seeing an empty box, the merchant was extremely embarrassed but said nothing.

When they returned home, he said: "Why did you give me an empty box? What happened to the other boxes of ingredients?"

"Master, you told me to arrive on time, regardless of what happened to the small boxes. I had to catch up with the speed of your horse. In doing so, the small boxes fell along the way."

"Next time you must pick up everything that falls to the ground," the merchant snapped.

"Yes, master," Thmenh Chey agreed.

Following his master's orders to the letter, the next day, Thmenh Chey stayed very close to the horse. It happened that the horse dropped dung from time to time. Thmenh Chey scooped up all the horse dung and stuffed it into the big box and, kicking a cloud of dust behind him, he tried his best to arrive on time. The merchant arrived first at the palace. He went to sit at his usual place among other officials. He did not see Thmenh Chey, who had arrived a few minutes late.

"Why are you late again?" the merchant demanded. "Bring me my betel nut box."

"Yes, master." Thmenh Chey pushed the box full of horse dung to his master, whose face became red with embarrassment and anger. He was outraged, but said nothing.

When they arrived back home, he shouted: "You fool! You are good for nothing! From now on, you must stay home and take care of the gardens. That's all you will have to do."

Thmenh Chey obeyed his master to the letter. He took care of the gardens. One day, the neighboring merchant's cattle came over and trampled his gardens. All but the trees were crushed. The merchant came by to inspect the disaster.

"Where have you been, boy? Why did you let those animals ruin my gardens?"

"Master, you told me to take care of the gardens. You never told me to chase the cattle away. Well, the gardens are still here, as you can see," he answered.

The merchant became silent. He thought to himself, *"This boy is really wicked. What can I use him for now?"* After some more thinking, he said: "From now on, you must take care of the herds. If anything happens to them, you will be whipped severely."

"I'll do anything you wish, Master. However, since I have no wife, I would like to call your cows my wives."

The merchant was quite perplexed by this extraordinary request, but just shrugged and went home. Off Thmenh Chey went to look after the merchant's herd in the fields. When other bulls came near his cows, he caught them and locked them up in the stable. By sunset, herdsmen came to the pasture looking for their animals. They were nowhere to be found. However, they heard some noise nearby. Directed by the noise, they found their bulls captive in Thmenh Chey's stable.

"What are you doing with our bulls?" they all yelled.

"Well, your bulls were trying to get to my wives. I was only protecting my integrity. I will give them back to you only if you pay me a ransom," said Thmenh Chey. Not happy with the answer, the herdsmen rushed to the merchant's house.

"Sir, your boy told us you had married him to all the cows. He confiscated all our forty bulls that approached his so-called wives. If we want them back, we will have to pay a great ransom. We are here to plead our cause and ask for restitution of our bulls without penalty."

The merchant sent for Thmenh Chey to appear before him and to explain his actions.

"What right do you have to confiscate other people's animals?" he asked Thmenh Chey.

"Dear Master, I requested that all cows be my wives and you agreed to it. These bulls came to my herd and tried to seduce my wives. I, too, have intended to bring this dispute to you. However, I'll accept any judgment you will make on this affair without protest."

"You are a vicious boy," snapped the merchant. "Return these animals to their owners immediately. From now on, you will not work in the fields anymore. I'll assign you to household chores only."

"At your command, Master," said Thmenh Chey.

One day, the merchant had invited businessmen to discuss some business affairs in a tent erected in front of his house. Due to the high intensity of the business, the meeting went on and on long after lunch time. The merchant's wife said to Thmenh Chey,"Go get my husband. It's lunch time. He must be very hungry by now."

Without hesitation, Thmenh Chey headed for the tent. When he arrived at the door, he crouched on the ground and yelled at the top of his lungs.

"Master, your wife wants you to come home for lunch." Seeing no one coming out of the tent, he went inside and shouted. "Your wife wants you to come home for lunch right now. It's long past lunch time."

The merchant was very embarrassed. Outside the tent he said angrily: "How dare you shout at me like that! Didn't you know I was in a big meeting? You must come closer and whisper in my ear in such a way that I am the only one to hear it."

"I just obeyed your wife's order," Thmenh Chey replied politely.

"Next time, if anyone sends for me, you must come closer and whisper the message, is that clear?"

"Yes, Master."

Sometime later, the merchant was working on his business

accounts in a small house beside the main house. Suddenly, a fire broke out in the main house. In a panic, his wife screamed to Thmenh Chey to go fetch her husband at once. The boy ran as fast as lightening toward the pavilion where his master was working. Out of breath, he approached the merchant and whispered a report of the incident.

"Speak louder, boy. I cannot hear you," the merchant said. Thmenh Chey continued to whisper in his ear that the house was on fire. The merchant still could not hear him.

"Louder, boy. What's the matter?"

"Your house is on fire."

Finally, the merchant understood. He told him to return to the house and try to save as many light objects as he could. After they had managed to put out the fire, the merchant gathered all his servants to provide an inventory of all the things they had saved. They had saved many precious things from the fire, but Thmenh Chey had saved only boxes of feathers.

"Why did you save these feathers?" the merchant demanded angrily.

"Master, you told me to save only light materials. There were no other items lighter than these feathers."

The merchant became speechless for a moment. He was thinking that Thmenh Chey had been playing tricks on him all along. However, he could not prove that Thmenh Chey had done these things intentionally. He had to find a way to punish the wicked boy.

"Go and find the culprit who caused the fire," the merchant said. "If you cannot find him, I will be sure it was you. I'll have no mercy on you."

Thmenh Chey disappeared. He walked straight to the kitchen, removed one of the charcoal stoves, put a chain around it, and dragged it as if it was the merchant's prisoner.

"Master, this is the evildoer that caused the fire."

The merchant was speechless at seeing such a hilarious staging. He did not know what else to say. Thmenh Chey always had the last word. He was thinking that if he kept the boy in his service, he might be ruined by him one day. The best way to solve this problem was to get rid of him by offering him to the King. The next day, unaware of his destiny, Thmenh Chey followed his master to the palace. When they both arrived at their destination, the merchant went directly to the throne room, prostrated himself before the King, and said:

"Your Majesty, forgive me for intruding upon you. But I have something very valuable that can be of service to your Majesty. Here is a young boy, named Thmenh Chey, of great intelligence. In my life, I have never come across anyone of his acumen. He has been in my service for several years now, and he always has the last word. It is of my humble opinion that I should not keep a boy of such ingenuity and cleverness as my servant. He could be of great service to the kingdom and to your Majesty if he becomes your servant."

The King asked Thmenh Chey to be brought in front of him.

"I was told that you could even trick the angel Tevoda [a Khmer mystic angel]," the King said. "If that is true, I want you to play a trick on me."

"Your Majesty, it would be impossible for me to play any trick on you without my precious 'trick book' which I left at my mother's house," said Thmenh Chey. "I could possibly not do anything without that book."

The King ordered one of his men to depart at once to the village and bring back that infamous book. The servant returned a few hours later, hands empty, informing the King there was no such book.

"Boy, no such book was found at your mother's house," said the king.

"That was the trick," replied Thmenh Chey.

The King could not help but laugh, and accepted Thmenh Chey as his servant from that day. When he began his service with the King, the boy was twelve years old.

THMENH CHEY AT THE PALACE

One beautiful sunny day, the King decided to go hunting with his retinue. High ranking dignitaries, concubines, soldiers, servants -- all on their adorned elephants glittering under the sun, all assembled around the king, ready to depart to the forest. The King, wanting to test Thmenh Chey's shrewdness and acumen, ordered him to carry all the food supplies and to arrive on time at the hunting grounds. For transportation, he would have an old elephant that could hardly stay steady on its legs. The mahout blew a hunting horn to excite the animals as a signal for departure. Without a word, Thmenh Chey mounted on the head of his old elephant at the tail of the convoy. With agonizing effort, his poor old elephant dragged its old feet one by one through the foliage of the trees, breaking branches that obstructed its path, trying to catch up with the procession ahead, but to no avail. Of course, Thmenh Chey and the animal lagged behind. When the King and his men arrived at the hunting grounds, they were nowhere to be found.

"Where is Thmenh Chey?" the King inquired. "I told him to get here on time or else he would be severely punished. As soon as he arrives, bring him to me," he told his men.

He then rested under a sacred banyan tree, surrounded by his train of attendants. Suddenly, one of his men came running and prostrated himself in front of him.

"Your Majesty, we see a shadow of Thmenh Chey and his elephant on the horizon. You can see for yourself. He is over there." The man pointed to the horizon.

The King rose from his seat, and cupped his right hand on his forehead to shadow his eyes from the glaring sun, so that he might have a better view of Thmenh Chey. What he saw was beyond his imagination. Thmenh Chey was standing on top of his elephant with a long bamboo pole. He pushed the pole to the ground as if he were on a boat floating in shallow water to help the elephant move forward. On the elephant's back was another bamboo pole used as a mast at the end of which a triangular white sheet was attached as a sail. The wind was blowing gently making the sail look like a real one on a ship trying to cross the sea to reach the farther land at the end of the horizon. He pushed and pushed the pole to the ground between bushes and trees, but it didn't matter what he did, his elephant was slower than molasses going up a hill on a cold winter day. Finally, they arrived at the hunting grounds, sweating profusely, where everybody was waiting and watching, dumbfounded by this odd, but ingenious invention. At the sight of this bizarre, but clever strategy to help his aged elephant move, the King burst out laughing and refrained from punishing the poor boy. As the days passed, the King's desire to beat Thmenh Chey's tricks never dimmed. He had devised a new plan for him. One day, he gathered his ministers again.

"Tomorrow afternoon, I want each of you to bring an egg and meet me at the lake. At my signal, each of you must dive into the water and resurface with an egg in your hand, making a 'cluck, cluck' sound like a young chicken that has just laid an egg."

Everyone understood what the King wanted them to do. At the set time, the King invited Thmenh Chey to come along carrying his betel nut box. The latter was unaware of the trick the king was playing on him. When they arrived at the lake, each minister took turns diving into the lake and resurfacing with an egg in his hand. Now it was Thmenh Chey's turn. He was told to dive and lay an egg like others. So he dove. With a big splash, he disappeared in the water. He moved around at the bottom of the lake enjoying himself with little fish roaming around him, thinking of a way to beat the odds. When he had enough, he came up to the surface and yelled: "Kocorico."

"Boy, where is your egg?"

"Your Majesty, I couldn't possibly lay an egg. I am the rooster."

Once again, the King was amazed by Thmenh Chey's quick answer. He did not say anything. After a wonderful afternoon at the lake, he told everyone to pack up and return to the palace. Many days passed. The King felt restless again. He organized another hunting trip. Under his instructions, his horsemen confiscated all horses within a two-mile radius and brought them to the royal stable. Everyone of his retinue was given a horse, except Thmenh Chey, and they all followed him to the hunting grounds in the forest a few miles away. He also instructed the equerry not to lend any horse to Thmenh Chey. The latter received the King's order to acquire one on his own and join the royal hunting cortege at the fixed destination. Since all horses in the neighborhood were confiscated, he took his chances and went to the royal stable. There the equerry threatened to whip him for daring to come and borrow one of the King's horses. There was no sign of a horse anywhere. Where could he find one? Suddenly, an idea came to him. He ran back to the palace game room where officials sometimes played chess. He grabbed one of the wooden horses, put it in his pocket, and rushed off like the wind to join the convoy, his feet kicking off plumes of dust behind him. Being young and an excellent runner, he arrived at almost the same time as others.

Seeing Thmenh Chey without a horse, the King asked: "Where is your horse, boy? I told you to acquire one."

Thmenh Chey gently pulled the wooden horse from his pocket and showed it to the King.

"Your Majesty, this is my horse."

The King was once more puzzled by the young man's astuteness and ability to provide such an amazing answer. However, his desire to get the best of Thmenh Chey's was always on his mind. He thought of another plan. He ordered his ministers to organize a cock fight, and to find him the best rooster for the championship. In doing so, he instructed everyone in the neighborhood neither to lend nor to sell a rooster to Thmenh Chey. The games were set one afternoon in the palace complex. News traveled fast. People brought their families and their best roosters. Many games were arranged, allowing everyone to enter the championships. Bets were also allowed, to arouse excitement about the games. Food and drink vendors of all kinds filled up the playing field. Music and dancing were provided as entertainment for the afternoon. People were shouting, screaming, booing, cheering, and laughing. It was an atmosphere of fun and relaxation.

Now it was time for the final championship - the King's rooster against Thmenh Chey's. The latter was not very concerned about the fight; he knew he would have the last word again. Knowing that people were forbidden to sell him a decent rooster, he went home. There he grabbed a very young chick that had just been hatched. He gently wrapped it in a soft handkerchief and brought it to the playground awaiting his turn to fight the King's rooster. The King then released his rooster. Everyone watched the upcoming game with intense curiosity.

"Now bring your rooster, boy," the King said.

Thmenh Chey unwrapped the young chick gently, and placed it in front of the rooster. The young chick, thinking the rooster was its mother, ran to take cover under the rooster's wings. The big rooster ran for his life outside of the playground.

"**Hay Eu, Hay Eu**! [Hurrah, hurrah!]" Thmenh Chey kept yelling several times, clapping his hands. "The King's rooster doesn't dare fight my chick. The King's rooster is no good. He is beaten. I win, I win!"

The King was more than furious. He was enraged. He told his ministers to forbid Thmenh Chey, thenceforth, to enter the palace. A few months passed. The King planned a festivity at the temple. He invited the chief monk to celebrate a religious ceremony at the palace temple. But restless Thmenh Chey was trying to find a way to enter the palace again. He sat at the corner of a gathering place where high-ranking officials usually met before entering the throne room. He said to one of them.

"When the time comes, the King will invite me to join the festivities again," he said.

"Oh yes? I doubt it," said one of the ministers ironically.

At the fixed date, Thmenh Chey intercepted the chief monk on his way to the palace.

"Dear Most Venerable Monk, I have something very important to tell you." Approaching closer to the monk, he whispered: "My hair is as beautiful as the tail of a peacock. Your bald head is better than my rear end." Then he moved back to his usual corner among the ministers.

"Do you want to bet?" he said loudly to one of the ministers. The King will ask for me in a few minutes.

They all booed and sneered at him. The monk was outraged by such a rude comment. He went straight to the King and asked that Thmenh Chey be punished for his insolent and disrespectful remarks. A few minutes later, the King's attendant rushed in and walked straight to Thmenh Chey.

"Follow me at once; the King wants to see you," he said.

Thmenh Chey winked at the ministers for not believing him, and without uttering a word, followed the attendant. When he arrived at the throne room, he prostrated himself in front of the King silently.

"Boy, the Venerable Chief Monk stated you insulted him by making disrespectful remarks -- is that true?" the King asked.

"Your August Majesty, I did say something; but nothing I said concerned or could be construed as an insult to the Venerable Monk. I said my hair looks like the tail of a peacock. In simple words, I meant that I am like a peacock that is allowed to live outside, but not in the palace. When I said his bald head is better than my rear end, I meant that he is lucky to be always welcome to the palace, whereas my bare rear end was forbidden to sit even on the floor of the palace."

The King was once more baffled and speechless at this reasoning. It was a logical answer. He did not find any insult from these comments to the Venerable Monk. He thought to himself: *"This boy always comes up with a clever answer to everything. I forbid him to enter the palace, he finds a way to come in without any difficulty with his sheer intelligence. So far, I have not been able to punish him for his tricks. I don't want to see his face anymore."*

So the word spread that the King did not wish to see Thmenh Chey's face anymore. A few months went by. A public announcement was made that the King would visit the market place on a certain date. The news went fast to Thmenh Chey whose house was located on the way to the market place. On the set day, he painted his rear end white, making two black holes as his eyes, a line for his nose and two others for his mouth. Having done that, he crouched at the window. When the King arrived at that level, he was puzzled to see such a bizarre thing. He climbed down from his royal carriage and went to inspect the weird object closer. When he realized it was Thmenh Chey's rear end, he went into a violent rage.

"How dare you show your rear end publicly to me, you insolent boy!" he shouted.

"Your Majesty, please forgive me. You have declared you do not wish to see my face again. That's why I want you to see another one by this window."

Again, and again, Thmenh Chey got off the hook, disarming the King's anger with his rational answers. His reputation as one of the most gifted and unbeatable Khmers spread all the way to China. The Chinese Emperor decided to send three enigmatic challenges to test the Khmer's ability to solve complex problems. He ordered his people to pick three melons from three different species. One contained one seed, the second two, and the third three. Having done that, he wrote a letter to the Khmer King as follows:

"Your Majesty, I have heard you possess a prophet in your kingdom. I am sending my ambassador along with five hundred ships full of treasures. There are also five hundred Chinese soldiers and civil servants on these ships. My ambassador will present to you three problems to be met. If your gifted young man can solve these enigmas, my soldiers and my ships, including their treasures and supplies, will belong to your kingdom. However, if you cannot solve these problems, your kingdom and your people will become slaves of China. My questions are very simple: *How many seeds are there in each of the three melons.*" The letter was sealed and given to the ambassador to be presented to the Khmer King.

As much as the King disliked Thmenh Chey, he needed his help. He said to him: "Boy, the Chinese Ambassador will bring three different kinds of melons tomorrow morning. If you can provide an accurate answer to the Chinese Emperor, I'll forget all my rancor toward you. If not, you will be put in prison for the rest of your life.

"Your Majesty should not be concerned about this simple question. I'll take care of it," he responded.

In reality, Thmenh Chey was worried. If he could not solve this enigma, he would lose his reputation as one of the cleverest Khmers in the kingdom. He had no inkling as to how many seed (s) each melon had. He went home, and lay down on the mat. He refused to eat the food his mother prepared for him. He lost his sleep. He said to himself: *"If I cannot solve this enigma, the King will kill me. No, I shall kill myself before that happens."* Decision made, he quietly left the house and walked toward the river to drown himself. The night came. It was pitch dark. From the banks, he could only see the dark, murky waters. He took a deep breath and plunged into the river. But the **Tevoda** (Khmer mystical angel) did not want him to die. He made several attempts, to no avail. Every time he dived, he was lifted up to the surface by an invisible hand. The current kept pushing him farther and farther toward the location where the Chinese ships were anchored. Suddenly, his body was pushed against the stern of the last Chinese ship. He heard some whispers from above. He grabbed the anchor, held his head above the water, and listened.

"I think we'd better find some more enigmas for this Khmer prophet, just in case he can solve this melon puzzle," said the Ambassador. " We know that there is one seed in the first melon, two seeds in the second, and three seeds in the third one. We must prepare more riddles or else we will lose our ships, our soldiers, and our treasures. First, let's make sure there is nobody listening to our conversation. " Having said that, the Ambassador and his counselor made a round of the deck. They did not see anyone near the ship, the coast was clear.

"Let's take a big piece of pork, continued the Ambassador. "The Khmer King has to find a way to eat the meat fresh for two years, without refrigeration, or salting process."

"How is that possible?" asked his counselor.

"It's easy. The pig must be killed in the evening of the last day of the year and cooked the next day of the New Year. That will make two years."

"It's amazing! Fantastic!"

The two Chinese officials were very happy with their devious new plans, and returned to their quarters for the rest of the night. Holding onto the anchor of the ship, Thmenh Chey did not miss one word of this most valuable conversation. His heart full of joy, he swam ashore and returned home to sleep to his heart's content for the rest of the night. The next day, fresh and full of confidence, he went to the palace to meet the Chinese dignitaries and the King. The throne room was full of people from both countries. They were anxious to see how Thmenh Chey was going to solve the melon riddles and the other two additional puzzles invented the night before. To the delight of the King and his entourage, Thmenh Chey had accurate answers to everything. As promised, the Chinese left the soldiers and the ships to the Khmer King, including all the treasures that had come with them, with the exception of one ship to take the Chinese Ambassador and his counselor back to China.

The King was grateful to Thmenh Chey for coming to his rescue. He gave him ample rewards for his deeds. However, the Chinese promised to come back and get even with the Khmer King with more challenges. Meanwhile, Thmenh Chey had gained the King's confidence, and became his counselor. Every now and then they played tricks on one another, but Thmenh Chey always had the last word. As a result, the King became very much concerned over his throne. He said to himself: *This young man seems to find answers for every difficult question. One day, he will take over my throne, my people, and all the wealth that comes with them. He's a threat to my power and my kingship."*

"Thmenh Chey, you have served me well over the years," the King said. "I am very grateful for your loyalty. But I think you would be much better off living on your own and being more independent. Go and establish yourself at the Great Lake. Make yourself a home and do whatever you want and have a happy life."

"At your command, your Majesty," he replied.

Before he left, he told the King's entourage that he had been appointed by the King to take care of the Great Lake.

"As a supreme commander of the region, I have a complete authority over the lake," he said. "Whoever disobeys my orders will be severely punished."

Off he went for the Great Lake. He encouraged villagers to build small habitations along the banks. They were allowed to fish for sustenance. Fish were bountiful. He instituted rules and regulations for trade. He imposed taxes on the boats that circulated on the lake to transport food and supplies, or as a means of transportation from one end to the other. He imposed taxes according to the size of the boats, the means and the purpose of the trips. He created a customs clearing house for merchant boats to declare their products and pay taxes, at different locations on the lake. A flag was erected at each customs house. He toured the lake, and gave names to its tributaries. These names still exist today.

At one of the extremities of the lake, water receded completely during the summer. He named it **Beng Phuok** – "Muddy Lake". On the Great Lake, he sowed green rice seed balls all over and made a public declaration that whoever used the lake, was allowed to do so; however, they should not disturb his floating rice balls. A fine of thirty ounces of gold would be imposed for any trespasser.

He named the Great Lake **Tonlé Sap** ("Sap" means "to sow" in Khmer). The name exists today. There was no way to cross the lake without making a dent to his rice balls. All this change did not receive a welcome response from merchant boats that used to roam around freely. They found the penalty too steep. The new policies created much discontent among the population. They filed a petition to the King.

The King sent for Thmenh Chey.

"Thmenh Chey, I sent you to the Great Lake to cultivate the land and live in peace, not to impose taxes on the people who live there. What do you have to say?"

"Your Majesty, we live in a kingdom without law and order, without a government. We must divide the land into regions or provinces. At the head of each region or province, we must designate a governor, and low level managers in charge of the administration of the town's responsibilities. We have to protect people from injustice. We have to build hospitals for the sick, and we have to collect taxes to pay for their upkeep and to support the welfare of the kingdom. It is not in my personal interest that I did all this. It's for the interest of our kingdom. For these reasons, I found the Great Lake as a starting point to implement my ideas."

"Well, you have great ideas Thmenh Chey," said the King. "Nevertheless, the taxes imposed on these people are too steep. Effective today, the penalty for infringing the law is a **Bat** [half an ounce]."

Instead, Thmenh Chey went to the temple and borrowed a Bat from a monk. (Monks use a deep wooden container called a Bat for their daily ritual rice collecting or **Benthibat** in the morning, throughout the village or town). Then he called for a town meeting.

"My dear friends, you all have heard of the new fine from the

King. From now on, use this Bat as a measurement for your fine." He showed them the deep wooden container used by the monks. "Just fill it up."

So everyone had to comply with the new measure, using the Bat. Only a very few could do it. The majority of the people were too poor to come up with enough gold to fill the Bat. Again, they were discontented. They all went back to the palace to complain about this new measurement. Addressing Thmenh Chey, the King said:

"I gave your orders to charge people a Bat, which is half an ounce of gold, not to use a monk's Bat as a measurement for the penalty! You understood what I meant. Instead of complying with my orders, you sow more discontent; you fan the flames of the people's anger against my person. If I continue to keep you in the kingdom, I will be ruined soon."

Having said that, he called forty of his most trusted henchmen, or **bourreaux** to take Thmenh Chey to the lake and kill him in front of the people of the Great Lake. The henchmen grabbed Thmenh Chey, bound his hands behind his back, and off they took him to the lake. There, the forty executioners threw him in a boat propelled with forty paddles. They steered the boat toward the middle of the lake. Thmenh Chey had no desire to die, just yet. He was scheming a way to cheat his guards.

"Hi **Bang Teang Aus Khnear** [Hi! big brothers]," he said. "I know I am going to die soon. However, I want to have a joyful death. There is no need to tie my hands behind my back. I cannot escape from all of you in the middle of the lake. We must enjoy ourselves one last time. Please untie my hands and I'll sing for you. After I finish a quatrain, you must all yell 'Hay Eu, Hay Eu!' [Hurrah, Hurrah, or Bravo, Bravo!]."

Having no doubt that the prisoner would not be able to escape, the henchmen untied his hands. Together they sang many songs. They sang the song of the moon, the song of the flowers, the song of beautiful girls. They sang anything that came to their minds. In the meantime, Thmenh Chey slipped to the rear of the boat. He continued to sing along with others. When he sang, "Thmenh Chey fell into the water," the henchmen gave a big chorus "Hay Eu, Hay Eu!" He repeated the quatrain and the chorus continued. Meanwhile, Thmenh Chey slipped into the water and swam as fast as he could to the river bank. One of the guards, seeing the trick of his prisoner, alerted the others. There was a melee among them. They blamed each other for their stupidity. Finally, they agreed to paddle back against the current where the prisoner slipped off the boat. It was too late. Thmenh Chey was nowhere to be found. They reported to the King that Thmenh Chey fell off the boat and was drowned.

"Never mind how he died, as long as he is dead," said the King.

Thmenh Chey was happy to find himself alive. He walked and walked until he reached a small village, and took refuge in a temple. Life had not been fair to him all these years. He wanted to do good deeds, but was punished for his actions. But he did not bear a grudge or feel resentment against anybody. He believed in fate. A moment of truth fell upon him. He decided to join the wisdom of Buddhism and become a monk. The news that the Khmer King had put his prophet to death traveled fast. It reached China. The Chinese Emperor called for a meeting with his ministers.

"The Khmer King put to death his most intelligent man. He was the only one who had the last word with us. Prepare some new riddles for the King. If he cannot solve them, we will take over the Khmer kingdom. Thmenh Chey is the only one who could challenge us."

Preparations were made for four ships to sail to the Khmer Kingdom. Each one was headed by a high ranking Chinese official who carried a sealed envelope containing its secret to be presented to the Khmer King.

The King felt a deep regret and sorrow for sending to death the only man who could save his kingdom from this new challenge. He said to himself: *"I sent Thmenh Chey to death by mistake. Only he could save me from this new embarrassment."*

As a monk, Thmenh Chey had sometimes wondered whether the King would recognize him, despite his yellow Buddhist robe, his bald head, and the shaved eyebrows imposed by the monastic rule. One morning, he grabbed a Bat and joined the other monks for the morning Benthibat rice collecting ritual in the royal palace community. As a good Buddhist, the King himself came down and offered food to the monks. When he arrived at the last monk, he saw a familiar face, but not sure who it was.

He mumbled to himself: "This monk looks like that trickster Thmenh Chey."

"Chey maybe, trickster no," Thmenh Chey whispered, loud enough for the King to hear.

Then he followed the others back to the temple. By the time the Chinese Emperor sent his emissaries to the Khmer kingdom, the King remembered having seen a monk who looked like Thmenh Chey. Maybe he was not dead after all, he thought. He sent his people to check every temple within a fifty mile radius to find that monk and bring him to the palace. This time, the King seemed genuinely ecstatic to see him.

"Venerable monk, are you still angry with me?" the King asked.

"Actually, you have my blessings," said Thmenh Chey.

The King told him about the new ordeal. He asked Thmenh

Chey whether he would accept the challenge one more time.

"His Majesty should not have to worry. We will not become a Chinese vassal," said Thmenh Chey.

The same day, through an elaborate religious ceremony, Thmenh Chey was relieved of his monastic vows and became a layman. The King gave him silk sampots (a traditional long skirt), silk shirts, a gold belt, and many other expensive pieces of clothing as required for a royal prophet.

"When do you think you will be ready to accept the challenge?" the King asked.

"I request three more days. In the meantime, I require Chinese ink, lots of white paper, a blackboard, and a basket full of live crabs be brought to me. I, too, will prepare some riddles for the Chinese. His Majesty should not be troubled over this."

Three days later, the Chinese prophets were invited to present their riddles. A big platform was built in the middle of the palace compound. Both parties sat facing one another. The Chief of the Chinese delegation pointed to the sky. Thmenh Chey pointed his forefinger to the sun. The Chinese pointed to the horizon. Thmenh Chey made a round circle with his right hand. The Chinese pointed his finger to the ground. Thmenh Chey pointed to himself.

The Chinese inquired: "What did we mean when we pointed to the sky?"

"You asked: What is there in the sky? And what did I mean when I pointed my forefinger to the sun?" Thmenh Chey countered.

"You meant that in the sky, there are the sun, the moon and many other stars. And what did I ask when I pointed to the horizon?"

"You wanted to know what is there at the end of the earth. And what was it when I made a circle over the horizon?"

"That meant we have the sea at the end of the horizon, and beyond is "**Mount Charkraval**," said the Chinese. (Mount Chakraval is the ultimate exterior mountain chains in Khmer legend.) " What did we mean when we pointed to the ground?"

"You wanted to know what is there on earth. What about my finger to myself?" asked Thmenh Chey.

"You said we have human beings like yourself," said the Chinese.

Everything seemed to be in order by both parties. The Chinese were amazed at the Khmer prophet, left, and retired to their ships. The next day, all came back for another round of challenges. The Chinese Chief opened his arms and made a round circle in front of him. Thmenh Chey bent back his elbows. The Chinese left without uttering a word.

The Supreme Chief of the Buddhist temple approached Thmenh Chey and inquired about the exchanged gestures, to which Thmenh Chey replied: "The Chinese made a circle with his hands. It represents a fish trap. I showed my elbow. It means that with this fish trap, we can catch fish as big as my elbow. The Chinese showed his five fingers. He meant that a big fish like that can be cut into five pieces. My single finger meant that, if we eat a piece a day, we could survive five days."

A minister approached Thmenh Chey and asked the same question. "When the Chinese made a circle with his arms, he wanted to convey to us that he would take over our kingdom," said Thmenh Chey. "By showing my elbow, I told him I would defend my kingdom with the force of my arm. When showing his five fingers, the Chinese informed us that they have many soldiers. With my only elbow, I made them understand that I am only one, but I have no fear."

Now the King sent for Thmenh Chey to give him some explanations of the debate.

"With the circle, the Chinese wanted to know what is there

on the four islands. I showed him my elbow, meaning that in the middle of the four islands was Mount Preah Somer. With his five fingers, they wanted to say that there were five buddhas. With my single finger, I told them that perhaps there had been five buddhas, but four of them were gone. There is only one and that had not yet been sanctified."

Pensive, the King said to himself, *"He gave three answers to three different people. We will never know which one is the truth."*

Lost in thought and concerned the king left. Before taking leave from the King, Thmenh Chey requested a blackboard, much white paper, some Chinese ink, and a basket full of live crabs. He went home with this collection of requirements for his tricks. The next day, he placed the blackboard in front of him, with white paper on it, and two bowls of Chinese ink in the middle of each side of the board. Then he released the crabs into the bowls of ink. The crabs, with their many legs blackened by the ink, crawled all over the white sheets of paper which Thmenh Chey religiously removed one by one, dried, and inserted them in a folder. He gave these sheets to some children, and told them to pretend to read by talking to one another loudly, anything they wanted to say when the Chinese officials arrived. The children obeyed. The Chinese officials tried to decipher sheet after sheet of paper with black crab leg designs, to no avail.

One of them asked, "What is this?"

"It's the alphabet that says: Cham, Pream," said Thmenh Chey. "If you cannot read these characters, then you cannot solve the challenge I have for you. Therefore, I win. I will take only the treasures from your ships. You can sail back with your soldiers; we do not need them. And please don't forget to tell the Chinese people to remember the name of Thmenh Chey."

Having said that, Thmenh Chey accompanied by his friends,

headed for the ships, seized all treasures, and carried them to the palace. The King was overjoyed to see so much treasure. He gave a great quantity back to Thmenh Chey such as china, porcelain, silk, silver, gold, and other many valuable things.

"I am very grateful for what you have done for me and our kingdom," said the King. "As a reward for your loyalty, I would like to offer you one of the most beautiful women in my palace as wife."

"Your Majesty, I'll accept only material gifts, but not the woman," said Thmenh Chey. "Because there are no women in the palace; there are only females. With your permission, I'll look for a wife myself. When I find her, I'll bring her to pay respects to your Majesty."

Thmenh Chey then left the palace with his many gifts in search of a wife. He went from village to village, but found none that he could call a "woman." He considered all of them he met on the way to be only females. One day, a stroke of good luck befell him. He arrived at a small village. He saw a young woman sitting on the steps of her house. Her name was **Suos**. He approached her.

"**Chumreap Suor Neang** [Good Day Miss!] Is there a woman in this village?" he inquired.

"Is there a man where you came from?" said she.

Thmenh Chey was very pleased with her answer. He said to himself: *"This is an intelligent woman."*

"Yes, where I came from, there is a man. Do you know his name?"

"Yes," she replied. "His name is Chey, meaning Victory. It's the most beautiful name on earth. And do you know the name of the woman you are talking to?"

"Yes, I know her name. She has the most beautiful name on earth. Her name is Suos. Please tell me, are you fearful?"

"No, I have no fear. And you?"

"No. Can you explain what it means when I asked you whether you were afraid?"

"You asked me whether I am married. Because if I were married, I would not be talking to a stranger for fear of violating Khmer tradition. Do you understand my question?"

"Yes, I understood your question. You asked me whether I were married. If I were, I would not be talking to another woman for fear of hurting my wife."

The exchange was a pleasant one. Thmenh Chey concluded that he finally had found the woman of his life. He went to her parents, offered them all the silk, silver, and other valuable gifts from the King, and asked them if he might marry their daughter. Not only were they overwhelmed by so many expensive gifts, but Suos' parents were also impressed by his good manners and his humility. He must be from an aristocratic family, they thought. They agreed to the marriage. It was a beautiful wedding that lasted three days. Music and classical dance were performed to entertain the many friends from the neighborhood. Abundant food, rice wine, and fruit were served. They tied the knot on the third day as prescribed by tradition. The couple lived happily thereafter.

Many months passed. One day, Thmenh Chey felt restless. He neatly wrote many debt agreements on white sheets of paper in his favor to all ministers of the court and other officials of the palace. The debt amount differed from one to another according to their ranks and their means. He took leave of his in-laws and his wife, telling them that he was going to collect his debts from the courtiers of the palace. There he found the usual crowd in the meeting room, waiting to be called by the King for an interview.

After a formal greeting to everyone he said: "Does anyone want to bet that I can make the King obey me?"

"Yeah, yeah," everyone jeered. "What's the amount of your bet?"

"The same as yours," he said. Then he gave each of them a sheet of the pre-prepared debt agreement to sign. He had them stamped and sealed by the royal seal. "Now please go to tell the King what our bet was."

The King was very hurt to hear of such impertinence and audacity from Thmenh Chey. He sent for him. The latter entered the throne room, prostrated himself before the King as required by tradition, and waited.

"Did you bet my ministers that you can make me obey you?"

"Yes, your Majesty. But I cannot command you, yet. Please turn your face around for one second." The King turned his head around as ordered.

He turned back to Thmenh Chey and said: "Now, try to give me some orders."

"Your Majesty, you just obeyed me by turning around. I would never order my King to carry heavy things on his head or his shoulders."

The last trick accomplished, he took leave of the King, and returned to the audience room to collect his winnings from the ministers. Happy once again to have tricked the King and won much money, he returned to his wife and lived happily as a rich man. After Thmenh Chey left, the King summoned all his ministers for a meeting. None of them were happy about the last trick played on them. They grew spiteful. For a long time, they resented Thmenh Chey for his intelligence, his shrewd tricks to gain access to the palace at will, and the favors shown to him by the King. Unanimously, they agreed that Thmenh Chey must be expelled from the country. He must be sent to China and die there. The Chinese, too, had a bone to pick with him. Once again, our prophet was forced to leave, this time to China. There he was left at an isolated beach with neither food nor money.

"Please tell my wife to be patient," he said to the King's sailors. "I promise the Chinese will send me back home within a few months."

The sailors promised to give the message to his wife. Our hero found himself once again stranded in a faraway land. He walked and walked. Finally, he reached a big city. He entered the first house that belonged to a prominent Chinese official. He humbly offered himself as a servant. Thinking he was an ordinary man, the Chinese man agreed. Thmenh Chey worked hard, saving all his wages every month. When he thought he had enough, he bought lots of rice, ground it, and turned it into flour. He invented a device that could cut the dough into long strips, and sold them in the market. (It was believed that the Chinese did not know how to make flour yet at the time, and that "Rice Noodles" were invented by Thmenh Chey.) It was a booming business. The news of his invention spread fast to the Emperor who summoned him to give him a demonstration of his new creation.

"What do you call this paste?" the Emperor inquired.

"Your Majesty, this is called "Rice Noodles. The only way for these rice noodles to taste better is to bend back your head, grab a handful of noodles and let them slip down your throat." At that time, it was forbidden to look at the face of the Emperor. Thmenh Chey wanted to see his face.

The Emperor did exactly what he was told. Seeing the Emperor's face, Thmenh Chey shouted: "I see the Emperor's face. It looks like a dog, whereas the Khmer King looks like a moon." (In Khmer legend, somebody with a moon face is supposed to have the most beautiful face on earth.)

The Chinese Emperor was outraged by the insult. He sent

Thmenh Chey to one of the coldest prisons, where prisoners would die within three days from the ruthless cold. There Thmenh Chey met a Chinese prisoner freshly arrived. To survive the deathly cold, he taught the Chinese to do some boxing. Every day, he and his companion practiced free boxing until they were exhausted. When their body temperature went down, they recommenced the games again. Three days later, the prison guard came back to check on the prisoners, hoping to see two dead bodies. Instead, he found both of them in good health, full of energy and practicing boxing.

He left, perplexed, and went to report to his superior. Meanwhile, a new idea tickled Thmenh Chey's mind. He taught his companion to build a big kite with long wings - a kite that could make a lamenting sound at night. He would check what way the wind would blow by kicking the dust. He held a spool of wire. His Chinese companion would run the kite high over his head. At his signal, the Chinese would let it go. Under a full moon, one saw a black dot in the sky, next to the moon. Or so it seemed. They flew their kite at night and hid it during the day. Every night, Chinese people, including the Emperor, heard a strange and scary sound from the sky. The strong wind sometimes made the kite whistle like a cry of a bird; sometimes it hummed a desperate lament, and sometimes it sounded like a moan or groan of somebody in pain. The Emperor was very concerned over these cries at night. He asked his ministers who confirmed that they too heard these agonizing sounds at night from far away in the sky. He summoned his astrologers about this bizarre event.

"Your Majesty, our nation is in danger," said one of them. "The whole population will be devoured by this animal where the noise came from, if we don't get rid of it." They continued to do some more calculations, and came to that conclusion.

"This bad luck that befell our country came from the Khmer

prophet. He was expelled by his own King and was left on our shore and was put in prison. Send him back home. If we can get rid of this man, everything will go back to normal," the astrologers said.

The Emperor was dumbfounded by the news. He had not known that the infamous Khmer prophet had landed in his country and caused this havoc. He sent for him.

"I am profoundly sorry to have inflicted on you such a shameful ordeal," he said. "I never thought for one moment that it was you whom I sent to prison. Please forgive me. I am offering you two hundred slaves, men and women, a hundred ships carrying all kinds of gifts, silk, silver, porcelain, and anything else you need. Just name it. Please accept these gifts and go back to your country."

"Your Majesty, I have no rancor toward you. The animal that threatened to kill your people is already dead," said Thmenh Chey.

"What do you call that animal?"

"It's called a 'Kite.'"

"Can you show me?"

"Yes, your Majesty. This animal does not have a head, mouth, ears or arms. But it has two horns that can make the distressing sound."

"That's very extraordinary. Can you fly it and make it cry again?"

So Thmenh Chey showed the Chinese Emperor and his people how to make a kite and how to run it. (It was believed that "Kite" flying was created by Thmenh Chey.) After the demonstration, Thmenh Chey, accompanied by Chinese slaves and one hundred ships full of treasure, sailed back to the Khmer kingdom to his wife. With his newly-acquired wealth, he built a beautiful home for his in-laws, and a beautiful mansion for himself, his wife, and his mother. Rumors spread that he had returned home with an enormous amount of treasures from China, including two hundred slaves and one hundred ships at his service. Nobody dared say anything malicious or disrespectful against him. One day, the King sent for him. He wanted to know what exactly happened after he was left on the Chinese beach. Thmenh Chey, without a grain of rancor against the King, told him everything, his creation of the "rice noodles," his time in prison that led him to invent the "kite," and the Chinese fear of the sound made by the flying object. He showed the King one of his kites. This practice of kite flying was Thmenh Chey's creation, according to the legend.

THMENH CHEY ON
HIS DEATH BED

Thmenh Chey lived a long, happy life with his wife. One day he fell sick. Knowing his time had come, he told his wife: "When I die, please bury me in a deep grave with bamboo sticks with sharp edges around my coffin. I beg you to obey my will. Now please go tell the King that I am dying and would like to talk to him."

The King came with his retinue. Thmenh Chey asked the King to approach him closer. He had something to tell him.

"Please come closer your Majesty. Put your ears against my lips." The King obeyed. "If you eat Trei Prourl, do not remove the skin. If you eat Trei Prah, do not throw away their gills. Trei Prah head is best served with lemon juice as a Pleah." Raising his voice for everyone to hear, Thmenh Chey continued: "Please, your Majesty, do not forget my recommendation."

The King was puzzled by this strange recommendation. His retinue wanted to know what was whispered to him. The King said that Thmenh Chey was just joking. Then he repeated word by word exactly what he was told. The dignitaries did not believe their ears. They thought Thmenh Chey had some more serious matters to tell the King, but the King did not want to pass them on. Thmenh Chey died a few days later. His body was buried according to his wishes.

When he was alive, he made as many friends as enemies, those whose money he took. These people sent their servants to ransack his tomb. Unfortunately, they were pricked by sharp bamboo sticks. They went home thinking Thmenh Chey was a mastermind until the end. He always had the last word, even after his death.

RABBIT, THE LAWYER
SOPHEA TONSAY

O nce upon a time, there lived a rabbit that possessed great intelligence. When he was young, he used to play beside a pond where the water was clear and fresh for drinking. Other animals that lived near the pond played there too. Nearby, there was a tall tree called **trach**. One day, cruel villagers came and chopped it down for firewood. There was nothing left of the tree except the big stump that still produced an abundant yellow sticky, gooey substance like resin. For the purpose of this story we will call our hero "Rabbit."

One morning, not knowing that the stump was covered with the sticky resin, Rabbit sat on it, peacefully enjoying the view of the pond and the sunrise. To his unpleasant surprise, Rabbit could not get up because the resin had glued him to the tree stump. He was very upset and thought he was going to die unless he could get off the tree stump.

Suddenly, an elephant appeared and walked in the direction of the pond. Rabbit said to himself: *"This elephant is going to save my life."* Rabbit then yelled: "Brother Elephant, don't drink that water. Preah Entrea has ordered me to guard the pond. Can't you see that I am sitting comfortably on my chair guarding it? If you dare to drink one drop of its water, I will trample your head and kill you."

At that, the elephant angrily responded: "You don't know what you are talking about. I don't drink your water. I drink the water that is in this pond."

"If you dare to drink this water, I am going to crush your head with my feet and kill you," replied Rabbit.

The elephant realized in a moment that this rabbit was very arrogant and disrespectful. *"How dare he crush my head when I am the biggest animal in the forest?"* he thought to himself. *"He pretends he is able to trample me. Well, I am going to show him who I am. I am going to reduce this little animal to marmalade. Nothing will be left of him, not even his bones."* With that, the elephant grabbed Rabbit with his trunk, pulled him off the tree stump and threw him on the ground.

In doing so, a part of Rabbit's behind was still stuck to the stump. However, Rabbit was free. In this way, the story tells us that the new bushy bunny tail that we see on rabbits today is the result of that accident. This new bushy tail replaced the old one that was left behind on the tree stump.

The elephant then decided to make soup out of the rabbit. Guessing the elephant's move, the rabbit said: "Big brother Elephant, I would like to die because I came to this Earth a thousand years ago, at the same time Preah Entrea created the world. I am old and tired of living. However, I feel it's only fair to tell you that my bones contain poisonous venom that could kill whoever comes into contact with it. If you hit me with your trunk, my bones will dig into your skin, and you will die. If you stamp on me, my bones will dig into your feet, and you will die. As for me, I cannot die. The only way to kill me is to find a very big thick brushy bush with lots of thorns and throw me into it."

Without hesitation, the elephant grabbed Rabbit for the second time and threw him far into that thorny bush. Rabbit did not hesitate for a moment and ran for his life onto the plain.

Thinking aloud, Rabbit said: "The next time the elephant sees a rabbit that he thinks he has killed very much alive, he will understand that I know more tricks than he does. He will be confused and ashamed of his own stupidity."

RABBIT AND THE JACKAL

During a dry season, a lonely jackal sadly ventured onto the plain looking for food. He arrived at an almost dry, very muddy pond. At the bottom of the muddy pond, he could see many miserable fish, crabs, and shrimp struggling to survive in the little water that remained.

"Today is my lucky day. More so than any other day," said Jackal aloud to himself.

A small shrimp, who had observed Jackal from the bottom of the pond, understood why Jackal was so cheerful. Rising closer to the edge of the pond, the shrimp said: "I know what you have in mind. You are looking for a delicious dinner. However, if you eat us as we are, we will not taste good. Our bodies are too full of mud. Besides, it could be dangerous to your health because we may be infected with terrible diseases."

"What shall I do then?" Jackal responded. "Do you have any suggestions? I want my meal as tasty as it can be."

Humbly, Shrimp replied: "If you take us to a bigger pond where there is plenty of water, we will be able to clean ourselves. Then we'll taste better and we will be an enjoyable, nutritious, and delicious meal for you."

"How am I going to transport all of you to the other pond? There are so many of you down here," said Jackal.

"Don't worry, big brother. If you listen to our guidance, you will be able to have a tasty dinner," said Shrimp.

"Sure, I am listening. Just tell me what I should do," answered Jackal.

"Please come, big brother, to the middle of the pond. Lie down, and we will climb on your back and hang onto your hair. Then you have to carry us to the other pond that has plenty of water. After we have cleansed ourselves in that water, you can eat us," responded Shrimp.

Jackal, who was greedy as well as stupid, followed Shrimp's instructions to the letter. Some of the shrimp, crabs, and fish from the dry pond climbed onto Jackal's back and hung on to his hair. Jackal took them to a bigger pond a mile away near the forest. When he arrived there, he gently entered into the water and released the animals from his back.

The shrimp, crabs, and fish, happy to find themselves in a pond with abundant clean water then said to Jackal: "Big brother Jackal, please go back to the dry pond and bring all our brothers and sisters before you eat us. We would like to be together."

So Jackal went back to the muddy pond, and lay down in it so that other fish, crabs, and shrimp could climb on his back. He then returned to the big pond to release them. On each of his return trips, he saw all the others waiting for him faithfully. Jackal was very confident that he would be able to eat them together when he had completed his task. He was really looking forward to a scrumptious dinner. He made many more trips. Finally, when it was certain that every brother and sister had been brought to the bigger pond, all of the shrimp, crabs, and fish disappeared in the deep water, leaving Jackal behind looking angrily at the water.

Realizing that he had been duped, Jackal got very angry. He called upon the other animals in the forest, small and big, to help him solve the problem. Among the animals that showed up were an elephant, a rhinoceros, a tiger, a lion, a python, snakes of all kinds, and birds of different species. They gathered near the bank of the pond as Jackal explained to them how he had been cheated by the fish, crabs, and shrimp. So that Jackal could eat them, he asked these animals to help him empty the pond.

The bad news had spread quickly. Having heard that Jackal was going to empty the pond, the fish, crabs, and shrimp feared for their lives.

"How can we stop these animals from emptying the pond?" they asked one another.

A small fish named **Trei Kranh** spoke up: "I have heard that there is a very intelligent rabbit. This rabbit can solve almost any problems in life. He has solved many an animal's problem as well as human beings' problems. Moreover, I have also heard that this rabbit is a very kind-hearted rabbit. He never turns down a request for help. We must look for him to resolve this delicate situation."

The fish, crabs, and shrimp were very delighted to hear this good news. They unanimously agreed that Trei Kranh should now depart at once to look for the wise rabbit.

As night fell upon the earth, our friend Rabbit set out in search of food. Soon after, he came upon the exhausted Trei Kranh. He asked: "Brother Kranh, you look exhausted. What brings you here?"

"Brother Rabbit, I have come a long way looking for you," replied Trei Kranh happily. "Our lives are in danger right now. We have heard that you always give a helping hand in an unfortunate situation. Please listen to our grief. Numerous animals, including an elephant, a rhinoceros, a tiger, snakes, and a multitude of other animals, including big birds, are right now getting ready to empty the pond where my brothers and sisters live. If you don't stop them now, we all will be eaten by the jackal. I implore you, brother Rabbit, to find a solution to save us from this catastrophe."

"Calm down, brother Kranh. Let me take care of it. Go back to your people and tell them not to worry," said Rabbit.

At these words, Trei Kranh returned to the pond where his brothers and sisters were anxiously waiting for him to announce the good news.

The next day, as the sun rose, Rabbit set out in the direction of the pond. There, he saw that many animals mentioned by Trei Kranh were busy emptying the pond. He then picked a big leaf from a tree. The leaf was half eaten by worms, and the other half showed traces of worms crawling on it. After having selected a higher ground at the edge of the pond, he lifted the leaf to his eyes and pretended to read it.

In a loud voice, so that he could be heard by all the animals, he read: "Brothers and sisters, listen to me. Preah Entrea will come to break the legs of the pelicans and the wings of the eagles, cut off the heads of the wolves, pull off the tusks of the elephant, chop off the head of the tiger, slice open the seal and slash the head of the python."

In Cambodian it said:
"Preah Entrea Lok Yeang Mok
Kach Choeung Trom
Promom Choeung Aurk
Kat Kbal Char Chaurk
Dauk Pluuk Damrei Sar
Kat Kbal A Kla
Oy Chroeuy Cheang Ké
Veas Pos A Phé
Kat Kbal A Thlan.

Before the rabbit finished his speech, the animals stopped what they were doing and ran for their lives. In the confusion, they stepped on one another and some of them were killed. The elephant, rhinoceros, and zebras stepped on the python, cutting him into three big pieces. A good number of animals that were killed during the confusion fell in the pond and became a big meal for the fish, crabs, and shrimp.

RABBIT AND THE TIGER

On his way home, Rabbit found a dead buffalo. The villagers had taken all its meat. Only the bones were left. He soaked his feet in the blood of the buffalo, put some on the tips of both his ears and continued his trip. A moment later, he saw a tiger. With an air of importance, he said:

"Brother Tiger, I just killed an elephant with my horns. And I have eaten all his meat. Just now, I have gored a buffalo. Look at my horns; they are still full of blood. I allowed the villagers to take all the meat. But there is still some left. Go and enjoy yourself."

"Your horns seem tender, brother Rabbit," replied the tiger. "How on earth did you kill an elephant and a buffalo with these soft horns?"

"My horns are extremely sharp," said Rabbit with pride.

Without saying anything, the tiger followed the rabbit to the dead buffalo and ate the remaining meat. The rabbit then said, "Brother Tiger, sit down. I am tired and I want to sleep for a while. Keep an eye on me while I am sleeping. When I wake up, we are going to find an elephant or a rhinoceros for dinner."

The tiger sat down next to the rabbit. The rabbit pretended to be asleep. The tiger, thinking the rabbit was soundly asleep, wanted to check on the sharpness of the rabbit's ears. He stretched one of his paws to feel the rabbit's ears to see whether they were really sharp and hard. The rabbit jumped to his feet and yelled to the tiger:

"Brother Tiger, what are you doing with your hand on my horns? I want to kill you right now. My horns are getting very itchy."

The frightened tiger sat down humbly without saying anything. The rabbit then went to sleep. When he woke up at sunset, he said: "Brother Tiger, go East in the direction of the forest, and I will go West. We will meet here tonight, at this very place. If you capture an elephant, bring me the tusks. If you capture a rhinoceros, bring me only the horns."

Having said that, both animals departed in opposite directions, looking for their dinner. En route, the rabbit found a big toad. He took the toad along with him to a nearby village. However, all houses in the village had been demolished. There was nothing left but a pile of bricks and plaster. Among these remains, the rabbit found a shard of a rice pot. Our rabbit was getting hungry and decided to look for some vegetables to eat. He found two stems of a vegetable called **Plauw Ang Kep** (Cambodian watercress). The stems of this vegetable are white and are shaped like miniature elephant tusks. He told the toad to hold the stems of the plant between his teeth.

"If the tiger asks you what these are, tell him that they are elephant tusks. As for the shard of this pot, tell him that it is the horn of a rhinoceros. Also tell him that I killed both animals today," the rabbit said to the toad.

Having said that, the rabbit put the shard of the pot in his mouth and continued his trip followed by the toad. When they arrived at the meeting place, they saw the tiger.

The tigers asked: "Brother Rabbit, did you have any luck today? As for me, I did not meet anyone."

"Ah, Brother Tiger, when I go hunting, I never return home

empty handed. Whatever my prey, I always find something."

The rabbit then put the shard of the pot in front of the tiger. The toad also took the two stems of the vegetable from his mouth.

"Brother Toad, please tell me what our brother Rabbit just took from his mouth," the tiger requested.

"Ah, Brother Tiger, that is called the horn of a rhinoceros," answered the toad.

"And what did you just take from your own mouth?" the tiger kept asking.

"These are the tusks of an elephant," said the toad.

"We have brought the leftovers of the animals that we killed today," the rabbit added. "Today, I was just happy to kill an elephant and a rhinoceros, but tomorrow, I am going to kill a tiger."

At these words, the tiger ran for his life. Later on, he found a hiding place at the top of a big tree. As night fell, the rabbit and the toad also found a hiding place to sleep. At dawn, both animals set out to look for the tiger. On their journey, they met a turtle and asked her to join them in the search for the tiger. They all followed the footprints left behind by the tiger. After a good while, they found the tiger hiding in the top of the tree.

The rabbit yelled out, "Good Morning, Brother Tiger. Don't you want to come down? We are going to cut down the tree anyway."

The toad then began to dig the earth around the tree. The rabbit called to the turtle: "Turtle, my big sister, you who used to topple a mountain with only one blow of your nose, come and help us cut down this tree."

The turtle gathered all her energy, and then threw herself against the trunk of the tree. But the tree did not move one inch.

"Big Brother Rabbit, the tree did not move," said the turtle.

To that, the rabbit replied: "The tree has been cut down, Big Sister Turtle."

Looking up at the tiger, the rabbit added, "Look up, Brother Tiger, the tree has been cut down."

The stupid tiger looked up and saw the clouds moving in the sky. He thought the tree had been brought down, jumped to the ground, and ran as fast as he could from the rabbit and his friends. A few miles later, he met a blacksmith who was sharpening a knife.

Still trembling with fear, the tiger said to the blacksmith: "Blacksmith, please help me. I am in fear. I am very afraid."

"What are you afraid of, tiger?" asked the blacksmith.

"Well, a rabbit, a toad, and a turtle, all with colossal strength, are in pursuit to kill me."

"Stay calm, tiger. Don't worry," said the blacksmith. "I will take care of the rabbit and the turtle. Their meat is delicious. They will make an excellent dinner for me tonight. In the meantime, hold these bellows for me. I want to finish my job of sharpening a knife."

The tiger calmed down a little bit, and tried to hold the bellows with his feet. But his feet were too small and his toes were too short. Consequently, he was not able to do what he was told to do. The blacksmith found a solid rope, bound the tiger to the chair and tied the tiger's feet to the handle of the bellows so that the tiger's other feet were free to hold the bellows and blow them. Suddenly, the rabbit, the toad and the turtle appeared. Seeing the tiger with a human being, the rabbit did not make a move. He sent the turtle inside the house.

"Hi Brother Tiger," yelled the turtle.

The tiger was trembling with fear when he heard the turtle. The tiger turned to the blacksmith. "Please help me, my good blacksmith, here they are," the tiger implored.

The blacksmith got out of his chair, grabbed the turtle and sat on it, and began to sharpen his knife.

From outside, the rabbit said loudly: "Look up, Big Sister Turtle." The turtle obeyed the rabbit's orders and looked up. Nobody was sure what the turtle saw. Anyway, with a big bite, the turtle bit something that made the blacksmith roll over in pain. The latter kept jumping up and down, trying to get rid of the turtle that firmly held on to something with her mouth. On the other side of the living room, the tiger was livid with fear.

A loud voice then echoed: "We are going to eat the tiger and the blacksmith. We will eat everything --not even bones will be left. We will devour them so fast that not even one drop of blood will have time to reach the floor."

The tiger was trembling with fear. He struggled with all his energy to untie himself from the chair. Since he was holding the bellows, his kicking, struggling, and blowing to disentangle himself from the chair produced sparks; his body then caught fire. The legends state that all tigers have yellow and black fur as a result of that incident. The tiger finally escaped. The blacksmith finally got rid of the turtle.

The three friends, the rabbit, the turtle, and the toad then decided to go back to their separate homes.

RABBIT, THE JUDGE

Back in the early ages, God created the sky, the earth, human beings, and animals. He also created millions of other things to fill the earth. He separated kingdoms and gave them to men. He also created races. It was believed that men and animals could converse with one another. The rabbit was known as a very intelligent animal and was used very often as arbitrator for disputes.

A farmer went to the marketplace. He had two baskets full of citrus fruits hung at the end of a long bamboo stick which he carried over his shoulders. The marketplace was located near the courthouse. When he arrived, he put down his heavy baskets on the floor, awaiting customers. Suddenly, he heard a grinding noise.

"What's making that noise?" the judge asked.

"Sir, it's the grinding wheels of an oxcart," the farmer replied.

"No, it's not an oxcart."

"Sure, it's an oxcart," the farmer insisted.

"If it's not an horse cart, what's your bet?"

"Sir, you can chop my head off. However, if it's an oxcart, what are you giving me?" the farmer asked.

The grinding machine came to a halt. The judge went over and asked the owner. "What do you call this machine?"

"It's called the steering wheel," he answered.

"And what is this?" the judge continued.

"It's a wheel."

"And this?" He pointed to another part of the wheel.

"It's the axle."

After many other questions, the owner of the machine described the axle, the hub, and the body of the cart to the judge. The latter still could not make sense of those instruments that made a cart.

He turned to the farmer and said angrily: "Come here so I can chop your head off. There is no such a thing as an oxcart."

The farmer, trembling with fear, implored the judge to grant him a few days to look for a lawyer.

"If my lawyer cannot convince you that this machine is an oxcart, I'll submit my head to you," he promised.

Off the farmer went to see the rabbit lawyer. We called him "Sophea Tonsay."

"Oh Great rabbit, I am fearful for my life," the farmer told the rabbit. He explained in detail what happened and begged the rabbit to save his life.

"Let's go see the judge. I'll take care of it," said Sophea Tonsay.

"Dear Great Judge, what did this miserable man do to you?" the rabbit inquired.

"My good Sophea Tonsay, this man was extremely impertinent. I heard a grinding noise that came toward us. This man came from nowhere and told me it's the noise of an oxcart. We made a bet -- if it wasn't an oxcart, he would give me his head; and if it was an oxcart, I'd give him money. Finally, the grinding machine arrived. We both went to explore the object of our curiosity. I did not see anything that resembles an oxcart. Thus, I won the bet."

"Oh Great Judge, you sure have won the bet. As a result, you can chop his head off," Sophea Tonsay replied.

The farmer was very upset and angry. He yelled at the rabbit: "I put my life in your hands, and now look at what you are doing to me! You've just invited the judge to chop off my head. What kind of help is that?"

The farmer, trembling uncontrollably from head to toe, did not dare to oppose the verdict. He bent down on all fours, ready to have his head chopped off by the judge. The latter lifted the sword, but the rabbit stopped him short.

"Great Judge, pay attention to what you are going to do." Pointing to the farmer's hair, the rabbit asked: "What is this?"

"It's the hair," said the judge.

"And this? What do you call it?"

"The skin," the judge replied.

"And what are you going to chop?"

"The head", the judge said suspiciously.

"Ah, Great Judge, when you made your bet, you saw everything but the oxcart. Now look at this object, I do not see the head either. I see the hair, the skin, and the flesh. If you can convince me that this is the head, I'll show you the oxcart."

It was decided that the judge and the farmer were even. Once again, Sophea Tonsay had resolved a dispute.

RABBIT WANTS TO EAT BANANAS

On a beautiful sunny morning, a rabbit, whom we call Tonsay, took a long, lazy stroll in the bushes and shrubs along the road to the village, exploring where he could find something to eat, and what it might be. He was starving because he hadn't eaten dinner the previous night. It was dangerous for him to be too close to the village and be seen by the people. There were also lots of dogs that he did not get along with. People liked his meat for soup or stew. Suddenly, he saw a farmer holding two baskets full of fruit at each end of a bamboo stick he carried over his shoulders. The farmer walked briskly, with the rhythm allowed by the weight of his baskets. His goal was to reach the marketplace, where he could sell his produce. One of the baskets contained ripe yellow bananas, the other, some vegetables from his gardens. The farmer always took this road to the market place.

Upon seeing the bananas, our rabbit said to himself: *"Today is my lucky day. I have to find a way to get to that basket."*

He kept running parallel to the road where the farmer headed. All of a sudden, he had a brilliant idea. He found a way to get to the basket without being noticed by the farmer. He ran faster, passing the farmer who, due to his heavy load of fruit and vegetables, did not pay attention to anything else but his baskets. Our rabbit then lay still in the middle of the road, his legs far apart, his belly facing the sky, pretending he was dead. When the farmer arrived and saw the rabbit, he said to himself:

"Thank you, Buddha, for sending me this freshly dead rabbit. This will bring me a few more **riels** *[Cambodian local money] than I anticipated from the sale of my produce. I can sell this rabbit for a good price, as its meat is very tender. People can make a scrumptious stew with it."*

He picked up the limp rabbit and threw it in the basket with the bananas. Our tricky friend the rabbit woke up from his pretended sleep, devouring one by one all the bananas of his dreams. When he finished, he jumped out of the basket and disappeared into the woods.

THE DEBTOR
AND THE CREDITOR

There once lived a man who borrowed money from a friend to set up a business. To simplify the story, we will call the debtor **Chor** and the creditor **Pin**. Chor drafted a loan agreement, dated the first day of the fifth moon, stating that principal and interest would be reimbursed at the time one could see two full moons. The friendly creditor, or Pin, not knowing Chor had more than one trick up his sleeve, signed the loan agreement without a second thought. On the contrary, Pin thought he was doing his friend a favor, and making a good business venture for himself. He could not wait to collect his money back, both principal and interest. After the duration of two full moons, he went to Chor's house to claim his money back as stated by the loan agreement. The debtor Chor refused to pay back, stating that he had to wait until he saw two full moons. Pin, not happy with this turn of event, drafted a complaint and rushed it to the court. The judge ordered the debtor to explain why he did not keep his promise to redeem his debts.

"Your honor, "said Chor," I am fully aware of my financial obligation toward this man. But this man did not understand the terms and conditions as stated in the loan agreement he signed. It says that he will be reimbursed in full, capital and interest, when there are two full moons. Honorable Judge, look at the sky now --do you see two full moons? I will pay him back at once, if you can confirm there are two full moons at this moment."

The judge looked up. Alas, he saw only one full moon. Scratching his bald head, he opined that the creditor should abide by the terms and conditions of the loan agreement. Pin was not very pleased with the verdict. He appealed the case and asked the judge to grant him three days to look for an arbitrator to solve his grievances. He went straight to see our rabbit lawyer "Tonsay," told him of his predicament, and said that he was very dissatisfied with the outcome of the verdict and needed help.

"Your problem is one of the simplest ones to solve," declared the rabbit. "Go and find some bamboo, some rope, and some wood with which we can build a beautiful raft. And don't forget palm leaves to make a roof."

The creditor obeyed. He went to the forest, cut palm leaves, tree leaves, and bamboo trunks. He took all the materials for the raft to the rabbit. Both of them went to work right away. A beautiful raft, covered by a thatched roof made of coconut and palm tree leaves, was completed that day.

"Now buy some rice wine," Tonsay said. "Ask your wife to make plenty of food and dessert, and bring it all to the raft tonight."

Pin ran back home, and ordered his wife to make a scrumptious meal for four people. That night the rabbit invited the Judge and Chor to the raft for dinner. The foursome enjoyed a festive banquet on the floating bamboo raft under a full moon.

After dinner, the rabbit casually turned to the judge and said: "Your honor, have you given the final verdict about the borrowed money yet?"

"Not yet," replied the judge. "However, in fairness to the

debtor, I think I'll have to abide by the terms and conditions of the loan agreement."

"May I question the defendant?" the rabbit asked.

"By all means," the judge replied suspiciously.

The rabbit then turned to Pin and said: "I understand that, according to the loan agreement, you are willing to fulfill your financial obligation -- not on the second full moon, but when there are two full moons, is that correct?"

"Yes," replied Chor, full of sarcasm. "If you can show me two full moons, I'll oblige at once."

Turning to the judge, the rabbit cried: "In that case, dear honorable judge, order this man to pay at once."

"But I only see one full moon," answered the judge.

"Look in the sky, honorable judge -- there is one full moon, is there not? And look down in the river, there is another full moon, is there not? Both moons are of the same size, they are round, golden and shining. There is no doubt about it. We have two full moons. The debtor must pay at once."

Caught in his own misjudgment, the judge ordered the debtor to pay not only the loan in full, capital and interest, but also two cows as compensation to the creditor.

THE STORY OF
TWO DEER HUNTERS

Sophea Tonsay's reputation as a wise arbitrator and lawyer had spread for miles around. He was called upon everywhere to settle any disputes.

Long ago, two friends in a small village, **Tun** and **Yim**, decided to go hunting one day. Early in the morning, they left their respective homes for the forest two miles away, each equipped with a net. When they arrived at their destination, they stopped and searched for a good place to set up their traps. Tun found a bush nearby. He spread his net that has a sort of bamboo spring around it and tied each end of the net to branches of a bush. When a deer ran into the net, the bamboo spring would close it like a trap. Yim, on the other hand, climbed up a big tree not far from Tun's net and set up his trap on top of a big branch of that tree. Having done so, the two hunters went home. Each one was convinced he would have a deer tomorrow for dinner.

The next day, very early in the morning, before sunrise, Yim left his home alone to check his trap. He saw a fresh dead deer caught in Tun's net in the bush. To his disappointment, he did not see any deer in his net set up on top of the tree. A vicious idea came to him. He removed the deer from Tun's net, took it to the top of the tree and tied it to the net, then climbed back down and went home to get some more sleep. After a good night's sleep, Tun went to Yim's house.

"Hey Yim, get up and let's go to check our nets," he called out.

The latter pretended that he was sound asleep and had forgotten about the time. He thanked his friend for waking him up. Both walked hastily to the forest. When they arrived at the spot, Tun was astonished to see no deer in his net, but when he looked up, he saw one on top of the tree. Looking closely at his trap, he saw some animal's struggling footprints on the ground, and his net was closed. He felt very suspicious about his friend:

"How the hell did that deer get to the top of the tree to be caught in that net?" he said to himself. *"I am sure the deer was mine, but Yim stole it from my net and placed it in his."*

They both went home quietly. Tun was very displeased by the findings. He drafted a complaint and took it to court. He told the judge he was suspicious about his friend Yim. The judge called the two friends to the bench, stating that there was no need to have a witness, that the case was good and clear.

"Any animal caught in the net belonged to the owner of that net," he said to Tun. "In addition, you have to pay the defendant, Yim, two more deer as compensation for his time and embarrassment."

The plaintiff was outraged by the sentence. He made an appeal by asking more time to look for a lawyer as an arbitrator. The judge granted him three more days, on the third day of which, at eight o'clock sharp, both parties must appear in court. Any party, who showed up late, even by one minute, would lose the case. Tun went home very angry and upset. He and his wife canvassed the whole village looking for some wise man who could help them win this case. On the second day, he came across "Sophea Tonsay."

"Pou [uncle], why do you look so upset and sad?" the rabbit inquired.

Tun related to Sophea Tonsay the whole dilemma. He was

convinced that his deer had been stolen by his friend, and that the judicial opinion he received from the judge was not fair and just.

The rabbit listened carefully and said: "Do not worry, Pou -- I'll take care of it tomorrow. Just leave it to me. However, if I help you win the case, what would be my reward?"

"I'll give you five riels," Tun replied.

"What am I supposed to do with the money?" Tonsay replied laughingly. "I want a whole branch of ripe bananas."

"It's a deal," said Tun.

"By the way, is there a dog at the courthouse?"

"Have no fear Sophea," Tun replied. "I'll make sure there won't be any dog when we arrive."

Tun and his wife went home, half-reassured, but pleased by the outcome of the meeting. The rabbit disappeared into the forest where he lived, preparing for a delightful meal of bananas tomorrow. The next day, before eight o'clock, Tun, with a branch of ripe bananas on his shoulders, walked briskly to the forest to fetch the rabbit. He was very edgy. The clock kept ticking. He kept telling Sophea Tonsay to hurry up. It was almost eight o'clock. To his dismay, the latter took his sweet time, eating a few bananas for breakfast before getting on the road. He was in no hurry to meet the deadline. Sometimes he stopped, listening to the birds singing, or smelling flowers along the road. Sometimes, he stopped to listen to a wailing wind or the rustling of trees. He walked a little bit, he ran a little bit, or he danced and pranced to greet the sunrise. There was no sign of alarm. It was past eight o'clock. As a matter of fact, close to nine o'clock. Tun scratched his head in despair; he mumbled to himself what a fool he was to trust a rabbit. There was no doubt he would lose the case.

Finally, they arrived at the court. Upon seeing them, the judge yelled at Tun: "What are you doing here at this time? And what is this rabbit doing in my court?"

Before Tun could open his mouth, Sophea Tonsay said: "This miserable man has asked me to be an arbitrator to defend his case."

"Did you forget that we agreed to convene at eight o'clock sharp?" the judge yelled at Tun. "I told you whoever showed up late, even by one minute, would lose the case," he continued.

"O Great Judge," Sophea Tonsay replied, "please do not blame this man. We left our home long before sunrise. However, I was so overwhelmed by the sight of beautiful nature that I could hardly move forward. You would not believe what I saw. Since the day I was born from my mother's womb, I have never seen anything like this. You, yourself, would be thunderstruck if you saw it."

"What kind of excitement have you seen that stopped you from arriving on time?" the judge asked.

"O Great Judge, you would not believe it if I told you what I saw. I saw a great number of fish climbing a tamarind tree to eat all the flowers. They kept climbing, higher and higher, until they reached the tip of the branches and not a single flower was left. I was dumbfounded by the sight."

"What on earth are you talking about, Sophea? You are a liar. There is no such thing. No fish can climb a tree."

"Did you say I lied to you, Great Judge? Our friend Yim told you he had caught a deer in the net he set up on top of a tall tree and you believed him. Have you seen a deer climbing a tree?

The judge had nothing to say, but admired Sophea Tonsay's wisdom. He reversed the verdict and ordered Yim to give Tun not one deer but two deer, in compensation for his time and embarrassment.

THE DREAM

There once lived a father and daughter in a village. The father was a rich man. His daughter was the most beautiful girl in the neighborhood. Although she had maids and servants to tend to her, she loved to work in her garden in front of the house. A father and son lived next door. They were very poor. Every day, the son went to work in the fields, passing by the garden of the lovely girl. He always stopped and stared at her for a while before he moved on. He was so infatuated with the girl that he sometimes lost sleep. One night he had a dream that he was married to the girl. They lived happily as husband and wife. He woke up with excitement. The dream was so real. He couldn't wait to tell his father about it. In the morning, he rushed into his father's room and said:

"Father, father, I had a wonderful dream. I dreamed that I married the girl next door and we lived happily together. Since I possessed her body as a husband, I want you to go to her father now and ask her to marry me."

The father told him it was only a dream, that he would never be able to afford such a rich girl. The son was so upset that he dressed up and went to the house next door himself. At the door, he asked to see the father of the lovely girl.

"What is all this about, young man?" the merchant inquired.

"Sir, I came to ask for your daughter's hand in marriage. I had a dream last night. She and I were married and had lived together as husband and wife. Therefore, you should give her permission to marry me."

The merchant was quite bewildered by this audacious poor young man. He said: "It was only a dream, young man. Go on with your life, and don't ever come back here again."

The young man was depressed. With an irritable sigh, he left the house and took the matter to court. He related his dream to the judge who summoned the merchant to appear in court the next day. He opined that since the young man had already enjoyed the pleasure of being the husband of his daughter, she should become his wife. The merchant was not satisfied with this judicious reasoning. He requested three days to look for a man of law to settle this dispute. Permission granted, the merchant hastily returned home, thinking all the way how he could find such a man. Suddenly, he heard a voice.

"Pou, why do you look so gloomy? Where are you going?" asked Sophea Tonsay.

"Well, Sophea, he replied, I am looking for an arbitrator to help me solve a big problem." He told the rabbit the whole matter of dispute and the verdict he had received.

"Don't worry, Pou," Sophea said. "I will take care of it. If I can help you win this case, what would be my reward?"

"Five riels," the merchant answered.

"What am I supposed to do with the money?" the rabbit replied, laughing loudly. "I just want a branch of ripe bananas."

"It's a deal," the merchant said.

The next day, both the merchant and Sophea Tonsay went to court to meet the judge. Upon seeing Sophea, whose reputation was known as a wise man, the judge inquired: "What wind has blown you here, Sophea?"

Honorable Judge, I am here to defend this man's cause." As soon as he said that, he dropped to the floor and fell soundly asleep. Everyone was stunned and confused to see such a behavior from Sophea.

The rabbit pretended to be asleep until the judge, who had other matters to tend to, grabbed him by the ears and said: "Wake up, Sophea. You came here to defend your friend, not to sleep in my court."

The rabbit rubbed his eyes vigorously as if he came out of a deep sleep, and declared with excitement, "O Great Judge, I am very grateful to you for waking me up. I just had a beautiful dream. In my dream, your wife and I had shared a voluptuous path together as husband and wife. Our souls were intertwined as one. We had enjoyed a mutual affection for one another. You must sacrifice your wife to me; I request she be my wife in real life."

"Insolent! How dare you humiliate me with such nonsense in public and in my court. It's only a dream. How dare you ask a well-known judge like me to give my wife of thirty years to you? Get out of here at once!" the judge screamed at Sophea Tonsay.

"Why is your honor so offended?" the rabbit asked. "That young man also had a dream, as I did. Didn't you, Great Judge, order the father to give his daughter away because of his ridiculous dream? Does it make sense that he should marry her, but I cannot have your wife? We have the same kind of dreams. Shouldn't the verdict be the same?"

The judge, embarrassed by his misjudgment, declared the father should be free to marry his daughter to anyone he liked.

Sources and Acknowledgements

Many thanks to William Nathaniel Harben for the story of Battambang. My thanks also go to my daughter Anne H. D. Carney for taking time to review and help with the pictures in this book, and for believing in what I am doing for the preservation of our culture, and to my son-in-law, Dr. John Ochsendorf, for his encouragement and support.

G. H. Monod, "Contes Khmères", traduit du Cambodgien, Edition Bossard, Paris 1922.

Every effort has been made to trace authors and copyright of "Phnom Bachey" and "Phnom Pros-Phnom Srey". I inherited a well torn book in Cambodian with no title, no authors, no dates, in a very poor condition, almost impossible to decipher the contents.

The rest of the stories are from memories.

Glossary

AThon: The affix "A" before the first name is commonly used in the Khmer language to call a young child of either gender. It could be a term of affection (in AVar Oeuy) or a harsh term toward the child when the caller is angry.

Ampil: Tamarind.

Apsara: Celestial dancers.

Bat: Old Khmer currency - pronounce "baat"

Bat: To lose, in Bat Dambang or lost stick.

Beng: A small lake.

Benthibat: Daily rice collecting rituals by Buddhist monks.

Chau: "Chau" is used before the first name to designate a young child. A term frequently used by grandparents to their grand children or by an elderly person toward a young child.

Chey: Victory or victorious.

Chumreab Suor: A polite greeting. The term goes for all times of the day. We don't have a specific for the morning, afternoon or night. Khmer people joined both hands when greeting friends or relatives.

Doeum Chrey: Sacred banyan tree.

Dambang: A stick. It usually designates a walking stick, or just a stick of certain length.

Eisei: A hermit who lives in solitude for religious reasons. In Khmer legend an "Eisei" possesses power to make or perform magical tasks.

Entrea: A mystic king from heaven.

Kampong: Riverbank.

Kaun: Child.

Kléng Srak: A species of a black bird in the family of crow with glossy black feathers. Its habitat is found in the tropical countries like Laos, Cambodia, Vietnam, Mayanmar. It emits a unique screeching vocal sound that is scary to listen to. It's a bad omen when this bird comes near your surroundings.

Kod: Each senior monk is allotted a small house in the Buddhist temple where he receives his followers.

Krahn: In Trei Krahn. It's a fish with dark scales that can move from one place to another with little water. In the rainy season, you can find these fish coming up to the banks of a small river or lake.

Kranhoung: A rare precious black tree.

Krapoeu: Crocodile.

Lak: Pronounce "Leeak". To hide.

Lok: Mister, or Mr. When affixed at the beginning of another word, i.e., in Lok Ta, it emphasizes respect.

Ma-Aum: A special cumin herb that grows abundantly in the rice fields. This aromatic herb is very commonly used in Khmer sour soups.

NeangKal: A plow. An old fashion apparatus farmers use to prepare the soil for the next seeding.

Neak Mean Bun: The compound word has three separate meanings: Neak (designation of a person of either gender); Mean (to have, or being rich); Bun (Bun alone means power, it could also mean festivity). In this instance, it refers to somebody who possesses power from above.

Neang: The term "Neang" preceding the first name usually addresses a girl or a young lady from upper class family.

Nen: Rank given to a novice or a monk of low denomination in the Buddhist practice.

Ngiet: Dried fish. Khmer people eat a lot of dried fish with rice soup, or just with plain rice.

Nuum: Cake.

Palaing: A pedestal on which a sacred object is placed.

Peou: The end of a family line. Usually it refers to the last child of the family, in Neang Peou.

Plauw Ang Kep: A perennial herb with white stalks similar to watercress that easily grows near banana trees, or any where the ground is wet. Used as salad.

Phlea: Fish salad. Beef is also used for Phlea.

Pou: When addressing an uncle or a middle age man you don't know too well, you affix "Pou" (meaning uncle) followed by his first name.

Prasat: Palace or monument.

Preah: The term usually precedes a celestial name, such as in Preah Entrea. Or it can precede a King's name, in Preah Bat ProhmKel.

Prek: When a river makes a fork.

Prohm: Derives from Brahmanism. It designates a supreme being from above.

Pros: Male gender.

Psar: Market, or marketplace.

Riel: Cambodian currency. The current rate is 4,000 riels to a dollar.

Samlar: Soup.

Sampot: A traditional Cambodian wrap-around long skirt for women. Men wear embroidered sampot during a traditional wedding

Sathei: Rich merchant.

Seus: A student.

Sdach Krahn: Refers to a king of a small kingdom.

Somer: Mount Preah Somer is a sacred mystic high mountain located in the center of the globe. Sometimes it's called "Someru", referring to Mount Meru.

Sophea: Title of a judge in the Khmer administration.

Srey: Female gender.

Ta: Grandfather. "Lot Ta" means Mr. Grandfather, a respectful accolade to call an elderly person.

Trapang: A small body of water, a pond.

Tevoda: A guardian angel from above.

Tonlé: A river, i.e., Tonlé Mekong.

Trei Prourl: A fresh water fish similar to rock fish but with soft scales. It's very delicious when stewed with sugar cane and fish sauce or made into sour soup.

Trei Prah: A very tasty fresh water fish with smooth skin that can reach two feet in length, similar to blue fish. Its egg is very sought after as a delicacy. The head of Trei Prah is well-known for fish salad. When salted and dried into "Ngiet", it can be preserved for a long period of time and very delicious when grilled.

Veal: Valley.

CPSIA information can be obtained
at www.ICGtesting.com
Printed in the USA
LVHW081729291221
707255LV00005B/376

9 781432 739379